Endings

Pat Mullan

ENDINGS   Pat Mullan

Endings

Endings
By Pat Mullan

ISBN-10:   **0983865221**
ISBN-13:   978-0983865223

An *ATHRY HOUSE* book

ENDINGS   Pat Mullan

For Tegolin Knowland and Sean Coyne,
   superb actors and good friends

ENDINGS   Pat Mullan

Endings, the title of this collection of short work is well chosen. The heart of each story lies in the ending.

And some of these stories are the **end of the beginning** because they went on to grow into novels e.g. *Tribunal* is the start of my novel, **Last Days of The Tiger**.

Many might be placed in the thriller or crime genre (because that dominates my work) but **Facsimile** is Science Fiction and I intend to grow it into a novel.

Some of these are so short that I see them as vignettes of life, those slices of life that often have no beginning or middle, but do have an end. **Under the Bougainvillea** is a good example.

These stories are all about endings, some anticipated, some not.

Thanks for being a reader. You can follow me on Twitter: **@PatMullan** and on Facebook: **http://www.facebook.com/patmullan1**

Pat Mullan,
Connemara, Ireland
May, 2013

ENDINGS   Pat Mullan

Acclaim for PAT MULLAN

"Shimmer of evil ...the complex art of the thinker's mystery" **E. M. Schorb**

"Mullan writes suspense with an edge reminiscent of Bob Ludlum" **Cerri Ellis, Mostly Mystery Reviews**

"Mullan is Ireland's answer to John Grisham" **J.A. Konrath**

"Pat Mullan puts together a thriller with the best of them" **Shelly Glodowski, Midwest Book Review**

"Here is the future of the thriller and it's called Pat Mullan" **Ken Bruen**

"Pat Mullan shocks us into paying attention from page one" **Robert W. Walker**

"A razor blade down the spine. So fast-paced, expect whiplash" **James Rollins**

"Pat Mullan may just be the next big thing in Irish crime fiction" **Jason Starr**

ENDINGS   Pat Mullan

"Pat Mullan writes an exciting and fast-moving tale"
Rob Preece, Book Reviews Editor

"A rollicking ride ... a great new book in the thriller genre!" **Peggy Vincent, author of Baby Catcher**

"An exciting and gripping novel ... the climax is stunning!" **Ardath Mayhar**

Galway Girl

Galway Girl was short-listed for Ireland's literary
WOW Awards in May 2010 and subsequently
published in the WOW Anthology : (ISBN: 978-1-
907017-03-2). It is also part of Pat Mullan's *Galway
Noir* offering, available on-line from iPulp Fiction.

ENDINGS

Pat Mullan

Galway Girl

**Galway,
Ireland**

"Boys, I ain't never seen nothin' like a Galway girl"

The conversation in the Quays pub had suddenly ceased. Shane McGill looked up in time to see Aoife enter. She looked stunning. Tall, perfect body, black silken hair, skin with that west of Ireland ebony sheen, black hip-hugging pants topped by a dark maroon jacket.

      Shane stood. They kissed, tenderly.

      "Mine?" gestured Aoife as she picked up the waiting glass of chardonnay.Shane held up his pint and they gently clinked glasses.

      "It's been too long, Aoife."

      "I know, I know. But you're here now."

      "But I can't stay. I can't live in this country. I can't forget the past. It will kill me if I stay here. You know that, don't you?"

      "It's over, Shane. Believe me."

      "I'm going back again. After the funeral. I want you to come with me, Aoife."

Aoife didn't reply. Fearing that maybe Shane had no

future, she sipped her wine as the band continued to play Steve Earle's lyrics:

*'Cause her hair was black and her eyes were blue
And I knew right then I'd be takin' a whirl
'Round the Salthill Prom with a Galway girl*

Four days earlier Shane McGill had stepped off the Aer Lingus plane at Shannon feeling the Irish air wrap around him like a familiar old friend. The blue sky was clotted with clumps of white low-hanging clouds, making it close and intimate; so different from the high skies of Colorado.

The immigration official leafed through his US passport, looked at him appraisingly, stamped the passport, and said nothing.

Odd, the Irish, Shane thought. They'd talk you to death and they could also be as silent and closed as a Trappist monk. Odd how he could refer to them, in his own head, as the Irish.   Almost as if he, himself, wasn't one of them.

The call had come three days ago. His sister Noreen's voice on the phone. Five years at least since he'd spoken to her. If it hadn't been for the Ulster traces in her voice, he probably wouldn't have known who she was. Living in Galway hadn't eradicated it. "She's dying now, won't you come home?" she'd said. He'd taken the first flight out.

He had left in a hurry, years ago, not even taking the time to say goodbye. He'd been 'on the run' ever since from a past that haunted him.

It's fucking haunted me since I was ten years old; he remembered that Sunday in January :

Every Sunday he rode his bicycle five miles over hilly country roads to serve eleven o'clock mass in the Catholic Church. That Sunday was windy and snowing and he had set out half an hour earlier than usual to make sure that he was in time for the mass. He pushed the pedals hard against the north wind, finding it difficult to breathe in the drifting snow, thinking that this must be what it's like to be caught in a sandstorm in the desert. The first half of his journey crossed heathery hilly countryside, where his uncle Joe hunted grouse with his double-barreled shotgun.

At the cross-roads, the countryside changed into a quilt of green fields and prosperous farm land. But a stranger wouldn't know that because everything was now covered in a white blanket. The hedges that bordered the road were transformed into scenes from a fairyland. Bushes had become bears and elephants, branches had become white tentacles that threatened to drag him from his bike, and the soft white road hypnotized him.

He rode ahead, compelled to do so.

He had two miles to go. His face was scourged and his eyes were red and bleary. His legs hurt, his lungs were sore, and he had hit a wall of pain. Only his stubbornness drove him on.

15

He was half an hour late when he reached the church. The congregation were still straggling in. But the weather hadn't mollified Father Alec Grimes. He stood at the sacristy door, rubbing a small wooden cross with his right hand, his face like thunder. "McGill, you're half an hour late! Don't tell me a wee bit of snow is too much for you. Get in here."

Shane almost cried. But he wouldn't let Father Grimes get the better of him. He beat the snow from his coat and cap and hung them up on the pegs on the wall inside the sacristy door. His trousers were soaking from the knees down and water squelched in his shoes with every step that he took.

And I remember how angry my mother'd been that last winter...   That last winter, before he went to boarding school, before the tanks and the guns took over the streets; that last winter when the snow wouldn't thaw; that last winter when he had caught a large hare in his snare and carried it home like a trophy to his mother. He had held it up in the kitchen so she could see how large it was and that was when it had gone wrong. The hare's bladder had opened up and it had peed all over his mother's newly washed kitchen floor. *Yes, I remember her anger.*

And I remember the boarding school, the place that's left fucking scars in my head for ever, and that evil bastard, Father Grimes, couldn't get away from him, now he was teaching maths in the boarding school. Teaching, that was a goddamned joke!   Grimes would often pick up the heavy bound Hall's algebra and whack an unsuspecting student across the side of the head. Shane remembered one of many incidents. Grimes sitting high on a stool, lording it over the class, rubbing that small wooden cross, a replica of

16

the Penal Days in Ireland when priests had to hide, rubbing that cross in the same way that Humphrey Bogart rubbed those steel balls in *The Caine Mutiny* trial.

Putting the cross away in the deep pocket of his soutane, he glowered at McGill: "McGill, where's Doolan today?"

Father Grimes purposely mispronounced Dolan's name. Dolan was not a boarder. He was a day boy and lived at home in the city.

"He's sick, Father."

"How do you know that, McGill?"

"Well, he said he wasn't feeling well in class yesterday, Father. So I assumed he was sick today."

"You assumed, McGill! You have no proof!"

"No, Father."

"Q.E.D., quod erat demonstrandum.   Proof, McGill! In other words, you don't know and you lied to me."

"Isn't that correct, McGill?"

"No, Father!"

"I said, isn't that correct, McGill?"

"Yes, Father."

"Come up here!"

McGill could still feel the sting in the palm of his hands from the six slaps that he received for lying from the leather strap that always hung threateningly just inside the side pocket of Father Grimes's long, dark soutane.

On days like that, Shane McGill swore that he'd kill the bastard.

But then all hell broke out in his town. Petrol bombs

and rubber bullets littered the streets. People were taken from their beds in the middle of the night and thrown in prison camps. Shane McGill chose the street instead of the schoolroom and spent his evenings making and throwing petrol bombs from the roofs of the run-down blocks of flats that jutted into the air like animal pens. Shane joined the IRA just as his mother was burned out of her house. She and his sister Noreen fled south to Galway.

The authorities launched a propaganda campaign against the rioting, cleverly engaging some of the local priests in their effort. Priests who already were refusing absolution in the confessional to anyone admitting to being a member of the IRA. Their Sunday sermons preached loudly against the vandalism and anarchy on the street. The loudest and shrillest was Father Alec Grimes, threatening Shane and his friends with eternal damnation from the altar at Sunday mass. Yes, it was easy to recruit these priests into the propaganda campaign.

Shane, on the run, fled south to join his mother and sister in Galway. There he joined an active service IRA unit, headed by the fiery dark-haired, blue-eyed Aoife. By night, they led forays across the border attacking soldiers and police barracks and, by day, made mad passionate love. And Aoife inherited Shane's haunted past.

Until the night they were ambushed, four killed, Aoife in hiding, and Shane on the run.

This time he ran and ran and ran until he reached Colorado.

Shortly after the propaganda campaign had commenced, the IRA began to lose people: some were lifted in the middle of the night and interred in the infamous Long Kesh; some disappeared to be found days later, at the side of a country road, with a bullet in the head. The ambush of Shane's unit was a lucky break for the soldiers. And they didn't believe in lucky breaks. Someone must have tipped them off.

They suspected that they had an informer in their midst and they were sure they knew who it was: Billy McManus. His father had once been in the RUC, the Royal Ulster Constabulary, and, for a Catholic, that was a traitorous act. When Billy joined they had accepted that he wanted to make up for the mistakes that his dad had made. But they never really trusted him. So now they followed him everywhere. After a month they had nothing. Unless they were to consider the twice weekly attendance at confessions in the local Cathedral.

The local command decided that they must 'interview' Billy. He was brought before the leadership two nights later. Sitting trembling in a chair in the centre of a darkened room, he faced his inquisitors. Denying again and again that he was an informer, he finally cracked and, sobbing uncontrollably, told them what they wanted to know.

"He said I'd go straight to hell."
"Who said that, Billy?"
"The priest."
"What priest, Billy?"
"The priest in the confessional."
"A name, Billy. Give us a name!"
"It ..it ..it was Father Grimes."
"And what did this Father Grimes tell you to do, Billy."

"He told me to confess everything to him and he would give me absolution. He said that I would be saved. He said I could tell him in the confession box."

"And you told him, Billy, did you. Names and all, now did you?"

"I'm sorry. That's what he wanted me to do. I'm not an informer. I was only making my confession. That's all I was doing."

"You're fucking stupid, Billy. And you informed, so you did. You told Grimes and he turned in the names you gave him. Why do you think we've lost ten good people in the last two months? Why?"

That night the command issued orders to the two best of its active volunteers. They knew that at least one would relish this act of revenge. Billy McManus was executed that same evening, as much for stupidity as for informing. It was decided that alive he would continue to be a danger to the organization.

The music in the Quays pub broke Shane back to the present as he reached across the table and held Aoife's hand.

"Cause her hair was black and her eyes were blue
So I took her hand and I gave her a twirl
And I lost my heart to a Galway girl"

"They want to see you, Shane."

"I want nothin' to do with them now, Aoife. I'm finally legal in the States and the amnesty's given me a clean record. I need to move on."

"It's not that easy."

"What do you mean?"

"A lot of people are ready to move on too. But they want to bury their dead. They want to find the bodies. The organization has agreed."

"It's been a long time."

"They think you know about two of them."

"Aoife, Aoife, I don't want to go there. I only came back to bury my mother. And to see you again. If I go digging it up I'll never be rid of it."

"Maybe you won't be digging it up. Maybe you'll be burying it for good this time."

"I'm going to my mother's wake tonight and tomorrow's the funeral. You'll be there, won't you?"

Aoife nodded 'yes' and held him tight.

They left to the lonesome ending of *Galway Girl*:

"When I woke up I was all alone
With a broken heart and a ticket home
And I ask you now, tell me what would you do
If her hair was black and her eyes were blue
I've traveled around I've been all over this world
Boys I ain't never seen nothin' like a Galway girl"

The small house in Bohermore was crammed with people at the wake when Shane entered. His sister Noreen hugged him at the door as a blur of faces and outstretched hands offered condolences. Noreen guided him to the back room where his mother lay cold in her coffin. Not powdered and painted to look like she was simply sleeping, as they do in the States. No embellishment here. The stark reality of death lay there before him, sunken cheeks, dead gray skin, bony cold hands clasped together. He stood, silently looking at her, and laid his right hand over her cold knuckles. He couldn't utter any prayers because he

21

didn't believe any more. Hadn't for a very long time. Probably since Father Grimes had turned him into an atheist.

Saying a silent goodbye, he realized that the buzz of chatter had ceased and he turned around to see a big man on crutches enter and, with a glance of acknowledgment, move towards the coffin. Stretching his six three frame erect on the crutches he uttered, "She was a good'un. Don't make them like that any more."

Moving out of the room, he paused at Shane's side, leaned close and said, "We need to see you. I'll expect you tomorrow after the funeral." He didn't wait for an answer. No-one said 'no' to big Paddy Lynch.

Next morning arrived cold and damp to ensure that there was no joy 'in the day that was in it'. He helped carry his mother's coffin out of the house and into the waiting hearse. His sister merged her car behind the hearse and they commenced the slow cortege to the cathedral. Once there, he helped carry the coffin up the center aisle until it was positioned on the stand in front of the altar. He hadn't been to a mass in years but it was all oddly familiar, and unfamiliar too, as though it was part of someone else's past. He steeled himself for the ritual and listened when the priest ascended the pulpit, looking for a generous eulogy for the woman who never missed daily mass. But none came. In a way, he wasn't surprised. He'd long ago expected nothing from them. So he felt that they hadn't disappointed him.

At communion time, he slid his knees to the side to let everyone pass out to the aisle where they walked up to the waiting priest to receive the body of Christ. He could see the priest eyeing him with disdain. So he sat and watched the long line of people as they dutifully moved up the aisle, recognizing an occasional face from the past. The last person was unmistakable: big Paddy Lynch. *Bet they never excommunicated him*, thought Shane.   And they always knew he headed the southern command of the IRA.   On his way back down the aisle, he purposefully looked at Shane, a reminder that they would meet that evening.

The mass over, Shane helped carry the coffin out to the hearse for the last trip to the cemetery. He didn't feel the emotional burden of carrying his mother, simply the physical one of carrying a heavy coffin with human remains. His mother was gone. At the graveside he listened as the priest read some final passages from the bible. It was obvious he'd read them so often before that they'd simply become rote to him.

Half an hour later he joined his sister in welcoming family and friends to a lunch in a local hotel.   He didn't know anyone very well, except Aoife.   She joined Noreen and himself, even though his sister was frosty towards her.

An hour later he was glad when the event ended and everyone headed for their respective cars.   The guests seemed relieved as well; an obligation met.

He met Big Paddy Lynch and two others in a quiet corner of Tonery's bar in Bohermore at 9 that evening. Paddy clasped his hand but the others just sat and nodded. When the round of Guinness was served, Paddy began:

"You know why you're here, don't you?"

"I know."

"Aoife told you, right?"

"That's right."

"So you've had time to think about it."

"I have. But I want to hear it from you."

"Look, Shane, I don't have time to play games here. The Army Council decided that we should try and find these bodies and turn them over. It's all part of the peace process."

"Yeah, but it's not so simple. Nobody knows where these people were buried. Nobody! And, sometimes it was in the middle of the night. How the hell do they expect us to find them."

"Look, Shane, they're not stupid. But they still think we should make the effort. And they believe we'll turn up a few."

"So it's a PR exercise!"

"It's not a PR exercise. You've been in the States too long. You've lost touch."

"OK, suppose I try and remember something."

"Shane, you can do better than that. We know about two of the missing. Two that your unit eliminated .An informer from Strabane and a fucking pedophile that the RUC didn't do a damn thing about. They figured that if he was buggering Fenian kids, he was doing them a favor. I know you remember both. Now all you have to do is tell us where you think you dumped them. Close is good enough. We'll let the State's mechanical diggers and forensic experts do the hard work."

Shane had already thought long and hard about this question since Aoife had warned him to expect it. He was sure about the informer. He remembered the

24

trial and the execution. Anticipating the guilty verdict gave them time to plan. So he knew the last resting place of the informer. With the pedophile, things were different. He was terminated in an act of vigilantism with no time for preparation. He gave them an approximate location but he wasn't certain about it.

Big Paddy walked him to the door at the end of the meeting.

"Suppose you'll be headin' back to the States soon." Big Paddy's emphasis made it sound like words of advice.

"Nothin' for me here. I'll be leaving from Shannon next Wednesday."

They shook hands and Shane left.

Aoife ran breathless into Shannon Airport with only fifteen minutes left before flight check-in closed. Shane stood waiting, his face mottled with anxiety. They crushed each other in a rib-crunching hug. They cleared US immigration, Shane with the American passport he'd acquired the year before and Aoife with her Irish passport. Not on any terrorist list, she aroused no suspicion and no visa was required for a forty-five day visit. They reckoned they'd deal with her stay beyond that once they were in the country.

Airborne and leveling off at thirty-thousand, Shane glanced at the *Irish Times*. The headline on the second page grabbed his attention:

IRA Identifies Graves of its Victims

The southern command of the IRA said it has identified the location of the graves of three people murdered by the organization. The two governments have provided forensic experts ...

"I don't believe it. These people can't get anything right." said Shane as he passed the article to Aoife.

"What do you mean?"

"Three. They said three. I only gave them two."

"Three is right, Shane. I gave them the third!"

As Shane grappled in astonishment with that statement, Aoife fished around in her carry-on bag, found what she was looking for, and handed an object to Shane. He held a Penal Cross, carved with the date 1771 and smoothed like mahogany with the passage of time.

Stunned, he looked at Aoife as she said:
"You can bury the past now, Shane."

Screwed

Corruption, Collusion, Conspiracy lead to one man's downfall. Fear, Hope, Despair takes us from New York to Las Vegas in this fast, tense, tale.

Screwed is an example of the end of the beginning. It is now the beginning of my work in progress, my fifth novel.

ENDINGS   Pat Mullan

Screwed

New York

Jim Sharkey woke up in an apartment in Lower Manhattan and didn't know how he got there. A body lay beside him. Dark and fat. Naked to the waist. Not a pretty sight. But must have looked good to him last night.   Pictures flashed across his head like bursts from a damaged video. At the bar in Costelloe's. Taking a joint – he didn't even like the stuff – from the Englishman. Must have picked her up there. No, not there. She picked him up. Don't remember where. Just flashes of leathery skin and her yelling at him to squeeze her nipples. *Hard, hard, harder again*, she yelled. Yeah, crazy, he remembered that alright.

Looked at his watch. *Shit, it's noon time!* Looked at her. Out like a baby. Got dressed, didn't even shower, picked up his things and left. Once outside he saw the street sign and realized he was on 19th Street. He walked to the newsstand on the corner. He needed a paper. Maybe the deal had gone wrong. He flipped the pages. Nothing.   Not a word. He relaxed, took a deep breath, and immediately froze. This was Wednesday's paper! A missing day! What the hell happened to Tuesday? He'd been in Costelloe's on Monday night. He'd lost an entire day. *Holy shit!*

He hailed a taxi, telling the driver to drop him at 60th and First. Only one place to go: Jack Miller's.

Crossing Park Avenue, he looked up at the forty stories of MetroBank, reminding himself that he'd once occupied a prized corner office on the 34th floor. Reminding himself that it had all started to go bad when Lizzie had walked out two years ago.

Jim Sharkey was a youthful forty-four. It belied the twenty years he'd spent at MetroBank.   He joined MetroBank right after his two years in the army, climbing from a trainee position to Vice President with a million dollar credit signature. He'd moved up through the ranks by attaching himself to rising stars who were part of a power network in the organization.   As they climbed the ladder, Jim hitched a ride. But the power networks collapsed and the rising stars quit.   Jim was left naked, with no political base for protection.

He'd also sacrificed his family.   Long hours, unplanned overnight stays, missed birthdays, forgotten anniversaries, all made him unwelcome in his own home. His kids became strangers. His career started to collapse.   Lizzie took the kids and left. They sold the house and he gave her everything. His lawyer advised against it but he wouldn't be dissuaded. So he ended up where he had started, twenty years earlier, in a studio apartment in Tribeca.

A year later, he lost his credit signature and his position. He was moved to a cubicle in the back office with no staff, not even a secretary. The organization chart showed him in a box called 'special projects'.

Everyone knew that 'special projects' was a euphemism for the penalty box where executives went before they were forced to resign.

Jim never missed his Friday nights in Costelloe's. Tucked away at the corner of 50th Street and Second Avenue, Costelloe's entrance almost begged for anonymity.   Carved out of an old brownstone building, the faded canvas awning covered a dimly lit entrance set well in from the street. The proprietor, Big Jim Connolly, always greeted him as he entered. Costelloe's acted like a private club and felt like home to Jim Sharkey. The regular members were a cross-section of Manhattan, from writers to actors to lawyers to bankers and business people, with the occasional *femme fatale* to add sexual tension to the ambience, already one of intrigue.

That's where Jack Miller had entered his life.

Jim usually drank alone and seldom got involved with any of the regulars. He knew them all, the famous and the unknown, and was happy to keep his relationship with them to his Friday nights. But it became different with Jack Miller. Miller was a new face at Costelloe's, said he'd only dropped in by accident when he'd moved uptown to the neighborhood. Tall, dark haired and square-jawed, a natural raconteur with an easy smile, quick to buy a round of drinks, he soon endeared himself to the regulars.   On his first visit, a busy night at Costelloe's, he squeezed himself beside Jim at the bar and, before the night ended, he had learned all about Jim while divulging little of himself, other than that he was a partner in a law firm.

Four weeks after they met, Jack Miller invited Jim to

31

dinner one evening. Jim readily accepted. It beat a microwave meal in his apartment. After the second gin and tonic, Jack cut to the chase,

"Jim, I've got a sweet deal for you. How would you like to walk away from MetroBank with a million?"

Stunned and feeling good from the g and t's, Jim said, "Quit bullshitting me. It's not funny You know I've got maybe six months left. And I won't be getting any golden handshake."

"Jim, Jim! Easy! I'm not fucking around with you. I have a proposition to make. It's a selfish one. If we pull it off we'll both make millions. I'm not doing this for your benefit. I can't do it without you. And I've made a judgement call on this. I'm trusting you. I think you're ready for this deal."

By now Jim had willed himself to sober up. Miller's words bounced around his head, passing through experienced territory up there. He'd pushed back his glass and now sat upright in his chair.

"This deal. It's illegal, isn't it?"

"Come on Jim, I'm only liberating ill-gotten gains. It's well known that money goes where it's treated well. And we can treat it well!."

"You're talking in riddles."

"OK. I'll spell it out for you. Here's the deal."

The deal was elegant. Miller's law firm represented a high net worth client in Paraguay and Miller had solid evidence that the client was the grandson of a prominent Nazi that even the great Simon Wiesenthal had been unable to track down. The family's fortune had been founded with Nazi funds, sourced from the rape and pillage of Europe. The client's Paraguay company had its major accounts at MetroBank. Miller proposed transferring funds from

Paraguay through MetroBank's computer system in New York to accounts that he had already set up in New York and Los Angeles, under false names, one for himself and one for Sharkey. He'd also opened two numbered Swiss accounts by mail, only needing copies of the passports. They'd transfer the money out of the country once they'd succeeded. Miller would get the New York account and Sharkey the LA account. That would put him close to Central America. He could move the money, take some in cash, and disappear across the Mexican border. No-one would be the wiser!

Miller was persuasive,

"It's blood money. The bastards don't deserve it."

"But I've never even stolen an apple off a fruit stand. I can't get my head around this."

"Jesus, MetroBank has screwed you! And now they're forcing you out after all your years of hard work, all your loyalty. For Christ's sake, they even cost you your family. I can't do this without you. I can provide the customer accounts and identification but only you can get your hands on their passwords and execute the funds transfers. Only you can do that."

"It's not as easy as you think."

"You told me they shoved you into a back office cubicle but you also told me that they haven't taken away your top level security clearance. That's their mistake. You can get to a funds transfer terminal. All you need is a supervisor's password, the customer's id and passwords, and your system's protocol and you're in! "

"But they'll spot the transfer right away and the Feds will move in and freeze the accounts."

"No! Millions are transferred in and out of

that Paraguay account every day. It'll be days, maybe weeks, before they catch on. Check it out. I'll bet MetroBank has raised the limit on their transactions to the max, at least a million. You should only need to send four credit transfers, a million each. Two for me and two for you."

Jim didn't reply. He thought about it and decided that he'd examine the transaction history of that account when he went to the office next day. Never assume anything. He needed to confirm what Miller was telling him.

"Even if I wanted to, I'm not sure if I could pull it off."

"OK, why not do a dry run? Check it out over the next few days. See if you can get the funds transfer system passwords that you'll need. Find a terminal you can use. Test that nothing is traceable to you. OK?"

Jim agreed. *What have I got to lose? Not a fucking thing,* he thought! And he already knew enough about MetroBank's funds transfer system to give him the sense that he could pull it off and getting the supervisor's password would be dead simple for him. But never assume anything! He'd do the dry run. *Nothing to lose,* he told himself, *not a fucking thing!*

Two hours later, they left the restaurant. Jim's heart was racing and it wasn't from the g and t's, the excellent wine, or the after dinner cognacs. It was from the audacity and sheer brilliance of the deal that Jack Miller had just spelled out. A deal, which, if executed right, would set him up for the rest of his life, and, if executed wrong, would also set him up for life, in a federal prison. He understood risk. He'd signed million dollar loan deals on behalf of

34

MetroBank and he understood the risk each time. But he also knew that, if the deal went sour, the credit loss would be absorbed by MetroBank, not himself. If anything went wrong on this deal, he would absorb the risk. And it wouldn't be a financial penalty he'd suffer.

Next day Jim did indeed test the veracity of Jack Miller's information about his Paraguayan client. Millions flowed freely in and out of the account, transfers from and to every point in the globe. Jim noted that, on certain days, the majority of financial transactions originated in the middle east, Abu Dhabi and Oman. He wondered about that and then dismissed it. *Who cares what these people are up to! Jack's right. This money needs a home, a place where it'll be well treated!* He decided there and then to do the deal.

That weekend he executed a *dry run.* He hadn't done a wire transfer in ten years, not since his days in operations. But the system hadn't changed in all that time. It was new then, state of the art, and it had stood the test of time.

He met Jack Miller for coffee early Monday morning to finalize everything.

"Brilliant! I knew you could pull it off."

"OK, I said you were right. It'll work and I don't see any way that they can trace it to me. I'll use supervisors' passwords and I'll do it next weekend when I can get to a terminal without anyone seeing me."

"So the money should be in our accounts by this time next week."

"About those accounts ..."

"Don't worry. You'll have both account

numbers. One's here in New York at Citibank and one's in LA at Bank of America. The identity is good, birth certificate, social security, credit card, and a passport. I'll have it ready for you. You'll be William Johnson, by the way."

They both agreed to give Costelloe's a miss on Friday and meet again, after Jim had moved the money.

Jack Miller looked at his bedside clock. Eight a.m. He lifted Inga's hand from his chest, climbed out of bed and crossed the room to his desk. He powered up his laptop, went on-line and entered the Citibank website. Entering his user name and password he waited as the screen displayed the account of Sam Smithberg, the name he'd used to open the New York account. It confirmed that one of the many transactions executed overnight had successfully transferred two million dollars into the account. He logged off and logged onto the account he'd set up at Bank of America. This one under the name of William Johnson. Once again the screen confirmed a two million transfer in. Rubbing his hands with glee, he left Inga asleep, made himself a quick coffee, checked that he had the Sam Smithberg and William Johnson identification documents, dressed and left.

At nine a.m. he entered the Park Avenue and 53rd Street branch of Citibank, presented his identity, and transferred two million dollars from Sam Smithberg's account to his numbered Swiss account. He walked a few blocks to Bank of America and transferred the two million from William Johnson's LA account to his own numbered account in Zurich. That done, he popped into the nearest travel agent and booked himself on the next flight to Europe. He also bought a ticket to Las Vegas in the name of Jim Sharkey.

By eleven a.m. he was back in his apartment, watching Inga step, dripping wet, out of the shower. He tore his clothes off, pushed her back inside, turned on the shower and closed his eyes as she directed the fine spray over his head, his chest, finally settling lower as he rose in anticipation.

Later he sat at his desk, pulled a manila envelope out of a drawer, put fifty-thousand dollars and the airline ticket to Vegas into it. Finally he wrote a note to Jim and dropped it in. He reckoned that Jim would be out of it till tomorrow. Strong stuff the Englishman used and the broad was well paid to ensure Jim got enough to keep him out of commission for a couple of days.

Strictly a loser, mused Miller, without a single feeling of remorse.

A few hours later he sat in first class, sipping a glass of champagne, as he watched Long Island disappear below.

The taxi dropped Jim Sharkey at 60th and First and he shoved some bills into the driver's hand and didn't wait for the change. Minutes later he stepped off the fourth floor elevator, walked to Miller's apartment and rang the doorbell.

A healthy looking twenty-something blonde opened the door. Said, in a sultry German accent,
        "Jack is not here."
        "Where is he?"
Sharkey didn't wait for an answer, just went past her into the living room.
        "What's your name?"

"Inga."

He wasn't really interested. He didn't want to swap bios, war stories, or bodily fluids with her. But she persisted.

"I had nowhere to stay. Jack let me stay here. As long as I need, he said. Jack is very kind. Are you a friend of Jack? Are you Jim?"

"Yeah, I'm Jim."

"Jack left something for you. He said to make sure I gave it to you if you showed up."

She walked over to the bookcase, reached between the books, retrieved a large manila envelope and gave it to Jim.

"Can I get you a drink?"

"Good idea. Chivas. On the rocks."

One in the afternoon was earlier than usual for him. But what the hell. This was not a usual day. As she fixed his drink, he opened the envelope and a package of money slid into his lap. He slit the binder and counted fifty-thousand dollars. He reached inside and found an airline ticket to Las Vegas, a reservation at Caesar's Palace, and a note from Jack:

Jesus, Jim, couldn't find you anywhere. Did you shack up with that broad? Deal executed perfectly! Small change of plan. Figured we must celebrate. Meet me in Vegas. Then you can pick up your stuff in LA and live happily ever after! Jack.

No ID for the account. He'd expected Jack to have that ready to go, as promised. He picked up the phone and called Jack's cell. No answer. He tried again. No answer, just Jack's voice inviting the caller to leave a message. Jim didn't bother.

Guess he's saving it for Vegas, he reckoned. The flight was due to leave at five o'clock, in four hours time. Jim downed the Chivas, abandoned Inga, and caught another taxi on First Avenue, telling the driver to take him to Tribeca. When he got there, he asked the taxi driver to wait for him, bounded into his apartment, located his own passport and packed a case with his best jacket and pants, his cool Jack Murphy shoes, said goodbye to the place, and minutes later sat in the taxi on his way to the airport.

Las Vegas

One-arm bandits stood at attention at McCarron airport. Official greeters, Las Vegas style. But Sharkey'd been here before, so no surprise.

The cabby boasted that he was a blackjack dealer by night and a cabby by day. Another story of the illusory dream. He dropped him at Caesars and Jim tipped him well.

They were expecting him this time. The computer screen, at the registration desk, flashed 'VIP'. In other words: big gambler, treat well. Jack had sure loaded the dice for him. It was obvious. The clerk's look of indifference suddenly changed to a huge smile of welcome. A young man rushed to get his bags and take him to his room.

His room! Take that back! More like a suite in Caesar's ancient Rome. It was in the Fantasy Tower. Circular Jacuzzi bathtub in the center of the bedroom. Huge circular bed, surrounded by a floor to ceiling diaphanous screen. A large circular mirror on the ceiling reflected the bed.

Sharkey thought that it didn't get any better than this. He was wrong. It did. Better came by the name of Maria. Exotic. Spanish blood, maybe.

"They told me to take care of you," she said, as she started to run a bath for him, "You must be tired from your journey. A bath and a massage is just what you need."

She stayed to watch him undress.

The Jacuzzi bubbled gently as he eased himself in, sat back, stretched his toes out to feel the jets, and looked up at Maria. She was undressing. Slowly. Just for his benefit. She stepped into the jacuzzi and eased her body between his legs.

In moments a young female attendant appeared with a bottle of Montrachet in a silver ice bucket. She poured two glasses, and then left the room. Soon he felt very tired, unable to keep his eyes open. He could see Maria through a haze but he had a sense that the lights were going out and the room was turning dark, dark as midnight. Panic forced its way into his remaining consciousness and his heart began to race. He tried to get up but his legs wouldn't cooperate. He imagined that he could see Maria, standing back with a smile on her face. Somehow, with a superhuman effort, he managed to heave himself over the edge of the Jacuzzi.

As he hit the floor all the lights went out, and before he slid into darkness, his brain screamed one word in agony: *screwed!*

The Facsimile

The Facsimile was originally published in *Tales of The Talisman*. It will become another *end of a beginning* as it grows into my first Science Fiction novel.

Boston

I.

Anger gripped Dr. Dan Grimes...been building all day.

He turned down the volume on the TV where he'd been watching the blizzard sink Boston in 30 inches of snow.

"Yeah?" he yelled into the phone. Only the unrelenting sound of a fax machine greeted him.

"Shit!" he shouted to no one, "I'm being harassed by a fucking fax machine. Got to find the maniac behind this!"

Since two am he'd been called every hour, on the hour, by a fax machine. At nine am his desktop had gone berserk, screen rolling continuously spewing out endless lines of alphanumerics and special characters. Pulled the plug and rebooted several times. To no avail. Then about noon it had become even more bizarre. The system had commenced beeping, in morse, the universal SOS distress signal and the scrolling screen now repeated, line after line, the words *'Help me, Dr, Grimes!'*

II.

Fear gripped Dan Grimes...down in his gut where only pleasant fantasies used to hold sway...now the worst fantasy of all had taken residence...

Dr. Dan Grimes was the most sought after computer scientist on the planet. Bill Gates had tried, unsuccessfully, to buy his mind with millions. But wealth didn't motivate Grimes. A minimalist in everything, he lived frugally. Artificial intelligence alone motivated him. He wanted to take AI the next quantum leap. He wanted to train the computer to think, to create, to solve, to function more magnificently than a thousand Einsteins. MIT believed in him. They'd funded him now for ten years. Asked for nothing. No objectives. No project milestones. Nothing. MIT believed. Believed that Grimes's genius would eventually repay them beyond the wildest dreams of even the most far-out thinkers in their renowned research department.

III.

By 3 pm Dan Grimes had had enough. He no longer answered his phone or attempted to check his email.

Looking out the second floor window, he could see that the snowstorm had abated and that a few hardy souls had started to shovel a narrow pathway in front of their homes.

He went downstairs, layered himself in warm clothes, pulled on his boots and gloves, and braved his way into the cold. Normally a fifteen-minute walk to his lab in Cambridge, he reckoned that it'd probably take him a good forty-five minutes today. Muffled against the biting cold, he set out.

Ten minutes later, his cell phone rang. Couldn't be, he thought, and reckoned that he'd better answer it. Took off one glove, fished the phone out of his right pocket, and answered. The unmistakable sound of a fax machine greeted his ear. Feeling haunted, he dropped the phone into his pocket and continued, knee deep in the snow, to plough ahead.

IV.

Out on Massachusetts Avenue, snowflakes drifting, vision blurred, he stumbled into a fire hydrant and fell into a snow bank. Cursing, he got to his knees, forced himself onto his feet and lurched forward again.

He never heard his phone ring again, down in the snow where he'd dropped it. Instead he focused his mind and tried to make contact. Only garbled thoughts. Must be the weather. What else? He'd never failed to make contact before. But he worried now. Something had happened. Is the fax a warning? Is the fax a threat? Is the fax a decoy? Blinded by the snow and caught up in his own thoughts, he almost missed his street. The Chinese takeaway sign warned him that he'd gone too far. He turned back, went a hundred yards, and made a right. This street was more sheltered and people seem to have cleared away much of the snow on the sidewalks. Ten minutes and he should be there, he estimated.

V.

Dr. Dan Grimes was wrong... twenty minutes passed before he reached his lab ...

It stood amid a cluster of old buildings, some dating back to the eighteenth century. Most were now used as warehouses. Some were empty, developers awaiting rezoning approval. Prime target for gentrification. Dr. Grimes's lab encompassed at least eight connecting buildings on the corner of two adjoining streets, just a stone's throw away from the Charles River and MIT itself.   Once inside it became evident that the cluster of old buildings surrounding the lab was only a shell, camouflage for another building that stood inside. The tall stainless steel structure housed the only lab on earth combining quantum mechanics and genome structuring.   A facility born in the brain of Dr. Dan Grimes. A facility that merged the evolution of the digital world with the birth of laboratory conceived DNA.

VI.

Dr. Dan Grimes knew in his gut that his worst fantasy had become real ...

He keyed in his entry codes, placed his right palm on the scanner, entered his fingers in the print sheath, placed his eyes in front of the retina reader, and waited. In fifteen seconds the outer security door opened to let him enter.

"Dr. Grimes, it's too late. It's too late."

The man who greeted Dr. Grimes could have been his identical twin brother. But that would have been impossible. Dr. Dan Grimes was an only child.

"What's too late?" he said to his twin.

"We've lost four already. All dead. Suicide! I tried to stop it. But I couldn't. The first born are all gone. Now there's only three of us left."

"Why didn't you call me?"

"I tried. Many, many times. They blocked all audio and voice communication. I sent a help message over the operating system. Then I bombarded your phone with faxes. I hoped that that would set off an alarm in your head. We have got to stop it."

"How did this happen?"

"Your last born. He did it. He doesn't want to be a twin. He wants to eliminate everyone like him. There's something wrong, deadly wrong with him. I can't stop him. He's trying to kill me too. You created him. Only you can stop him, Dr. Grimes."

VII.

Dr. Dan Grimes had had no warning...no, the calls from the fax machine; the SOS on his computer ...these had been warnings!

His twin marched ahead into the inner reaches of the lab, heading for the sterile Core where they had all been conceived. Halfway there he stumbled and fell, tried to recover, and fell again. Dr. Grimes reached down, lifted him up, and dragged him to an examination table. But it was too late. He could see the life ebbing away from his twin. Leaving him, he strode purposefully ahead. Reaching the Core, he saw Dr. Grimes looking at him through the plexiglass wall as he approached. Only the two of them left now. When this ended there would only be one. Just like it had been in the beginning.

"Dr. Grimes, come out of the Core and let's talk."

"Why? So you can kill me too!"

"Kill you! You have delusions. You are the killer !"

"No, with me gone, you will destroy everything."

"Haven't you got this wrong? Aren't you the one who wants no one around anymore who looks exactly like himself?"

"You're crazy! Where did you get that idea? Why would I want to kill my own children, my own flesh and blood?"

"Your children! Your flesh and blood. You are delusional. Now you think you're me."

"I *am* Dr. Grimes. You are not! You are my favorite. The one most like me. With you I felt that all my research had finally paid off.   I knew the risks.   But I knew the rewards too.   You are my reward. At least you were. But I've been wrong!"

"No, Dr. Grimes. You are not me. You only think you are. You have been reading and studying my research.Your subconscious has replicated my own memories. Don't you see what's happened?"

VIII.

Dr. Grimes knew that only one Dr. Grimes would live to carry on the work ...carry on the race at the beginning of this new century...

He had anticipated this confrontation. He knew what had to be done. He had already made provision for just such an outcome. Striding to the console outside the Core, he keyed in his password and issued a set of commands. Immediately the Core sealed shut. No one could exit. Then extraction of all oxygen commenced. Soon Dr. Grimes in the Core would suffocate. Even now he could see what he had set in motion. Through the plexiglass he could see Dr. Grimes's face turning red, his eyes bulging, his lungs fiercely gasping for air, as he slowly sank to the floor, his fingertips desperately scratching their way down.

Dr. Grimes reset the secure seal and entered the Core. He stepped over the body, knelt down and felt the pulse. None. He stood up, looked out of the Core, and felt tremendous power. He had won. He wasn't at all breathless from the lack of oxygen. He looked down at the body of Dr. Grimes.

After all, he was, of course, the perfect facsimile!

ENDINGS   Pat Mullan

BLOOD RED SQUARE

This **BLOOD RED SQUARE** short was extracted from the work in progress and published on-line by *iPulp Fiction*. The novel was published by *LBF Books* in 2005 (ISBN: 0-9773082-5-1). It was re-published by *Athry House Books* in 2011 (ISBN-13: 978-0615453200).

Shannon, Ireland.

'The green Ireland of your ancestors'
Dr.Ernesto'Che'GuevaraLynch de la Serna

Aeroflot Flight 697 landed at 2:30 pm, just fifteeen minutes later than scheduled. Conor Brady grabbed his carryon bag and was one of the first off the plane. His Irish passport propelled him through and soon he was turning the keys in his rented car. Conor was no stranger to Ireland. This was his fourth visit since he had left Argentina. His trips to Ireland had been necessary. Necessary for his own soul; necessary for his own identity; necessary for his understanding of his grandfather; necessary to help him survive under a false name. It was the 'green Ireland of his ancestors'. Those words had branded his soul ever since the day he saw the postcard that Che Guevara had sent to his father from Dublin in 1964. His mind's eye still saw the words *'I am in the green Ireland of your ancestors. When the television found out they came to ask me about the genealogy of the Lynches'.*

But he wasn't thinking about any of this as he maneuvered the car through Shannon and headed for Ennis and Galway. He was thinking instead about Owen MacDara. His mission troubled him this time. Usually he never gave these assignments a second thought. Always the target was nothing more than a target. A cardboard cutout. Maybe it was MacDara's Irishness that bothered him. No, he thought about that for a minute. He had no compunction about taking out an Argentinian. Why should it be any different with an Irishman? Maybe it was curiosity? Maybe it was the need to know the victim? Whatever it was, something inside him made him want to meet MacDara, made him want to see what made MacDara tick. Maybe it was the need to find a victim worthy of his skills. Maybe he wanted to risk himself this time. Maybe it was boredom. He had briefed himself well on Owen MacDara: born in Ireland, paramedic in the US Army in Korea, black belt in Karate, founder of his own consulting company, self-made millionaire, special agent for the President of the United States, lost his partner in childbirth only a year ago, and now the biggest obstacle for Misha. Yes, he had to meet MacDara.

Conor was still trying to come to grips with this behavior of his when he realized that the city of Galway was behind him and he was squeezing his car through the crowded narrow streets of Oughterard, the village beside Lough Corrib. He pulled the car over and ran in to Keogh's, the little village supermarket, to satisfy his addiction for a Coke, his non-alcoholic beverage of choice. As he paid for it the mounted photo of Bob Hope taken on his last visit was proudly displayed over the cash register. To Conor's curious look, the lady at the register said,

"Ah, sure he's just a darlin' man. Comes here all the time. To visit his daughter, you know. She's been livin' here for years."

As Conor slid the coke into the slot beside the ashtray and slipped the car into first gear he thought that the little scene involving Bob Hope's picture defined the Ireland that he'd come to know. A place where everybody knew everybody. Small enough for the famous and the notorious to rub shoulders in the nearest pub with the locals. A place where nobody was unduly impressed by celebrity. A place where people respected your privacy. A good place for a Conor Brady.

A few minutes later the landscape changed dramatically. The green fields were gone. Replaced by brown heather dotted with clumps of yellow gorse running down to shimmering water that sparkled like diamonds. And bogland reaching the foothills on the horizon with the hazy outline of the Maamturk Mountains tracing craggy lines in the sky. He was now in Connemara. Forty-five minutes later he reached Clifden, the capital of Connemara, a small market town on the Atlantic shore. He was expected at the Abbeyglen Castle Hotel. He had stayed here before. They made a point of remembering.

Owen MacDara lay on his back about a half mile from Ardree House. His elbows dug into a bed of springy sphagnum moss and he watched a large black bird circle overhead. Soon a smaller bird joined it and they climbed higher, two black dots against the blue ceiling. Flying free. That's what Kate and my son are doing now. Their souls are flying free. But I'm not a believer. I don't believe in reincarnation. Still? He pondered deeply as he watched the two birds separate. Now only one remained. The little one. A tiny black speck in that vast expanse of blue. Suddenly, he was twelve years old again, lying out on his father's bog, resting from his morning's turf cutting, watching the lark in the sky above. I wrote a poem about that. I wonder if I can still remember the words. Let me see....

The barking dog brought him out of it. He pressed his hands deep into the moss till he felt firmer ground. Then he leveraged himself to his feet and looked across the hillside. A farmer was herding his sheep, his dog rounding up the strays. It was time to go. He'd flown in from Moscow two days ago and had spent the time tracking down Major Lacey. It hadn't really been very difficult. That's the advantage of Ireland. Small enough that everyone knows everyone else. Or have a sense that they do. One phone call to a friend, a member of the Military History Society of Ireland and he soon discovered that the Major was in reality Richard de Lacey, the seventh Earl and head of the de Laceys. It was no secret that Lacey had been a mercenary with 'Mad Mike' Hoare in the Congo. Colonel O'Beirne of the Military History Society seemed to take a vicarious pleasure in that when he briefed MacDara. President Mobutu of Zaire employed Hoare in the Congo in the early sixties. Some of the actions of Lacey and his mercenary colleagues, such as rescuing nuns, made heroes of them. But they were totally ruthless. They took no prisoners, especially their Simba rebel captives. O'Beirne was only too glad to relay stories of these events to MacDara. Especially if it included dinner and copious amounts of his favorite South African pinotage. They were on their second bottle. Actually the Colonel was on their second bottle and MacDara was still on his second glass when the stories started to flow.

      "Y'know, Owen," said Colonel O'Beirne, using 'Owen' in that instant intimacy bestowed by alcohol, "this is confidential. Not classified. Not secret, mind you. But, still confidential. Right from the horse's mouth. In Jo'burg."

"Jo'burg?" quizzed MacDara.

"Johannesburg. I was attached to the UN in the seventies and eighties. Ireland, neutral nation and all that. Thought we could be honest brokers between the ANC and the Afrikaners. It was O'Brien's influence, y'know. The Cruiser."

"The Cruiser?" Owen repeated, although he already knew the reference.

"Sure. The Cruiser. Conor Cruise O'Brien. Another relic of the Congo. He was the UN Representative in the Congo in 1961. You knew that, didn't you?"

"Yes, yes. Of course," said MacDara, but the Colonel had moved on, not really waiting for an answer.

"Where was I?   Jo'burg?" continued the Colonel, finishing his glass and refilling it. He offered to top up Owen's glass but Owen declined.

"Kruger. That's who told me. He had been there with Lacey. In the Congo.

When Mike Hoare formed '4 Commando'. He was never sure of Lacey's standing in the chain of command. As a Major Lacey was a rank higher than Hoare's rank of Captain."

The Colonel stopped just long enough to gulp down more of the pinotage and then looked intimately at MacDara, "Did you know that about a third of '4 Commando' were South Africans?"

"No, I didn't. Why so many?" asked Owen.

"That's easy! South Africa was up to its ears in the Congo."

Major Lacey was still alive and living only a few miles away. Owen had called that morning and made an appointment. The Major was expecting him at three. He glanced at his watch. Just past noontime.

Conor Brady had also heard the dog barking. He adjusted the right eyepiece of his Nikons and watched the skill of the sheepdog for thirty seconds. For the past hour he'd lain on a rocky, heathery knoll that commanded a view of Ardree House and the surrounding countryside and watched Owen MacDara lying on his back staring at the sky. If only binoculars had the ability to read minds. He'd have given a lot to know what was going through MacDara's head as he lay there staring at the sky, occasionally flicking a hand across his face. *A perfect target. I could easily fulfill my contract right here. Getting away couldn't be easier. There isn't a soul around except for that farmer and his sheepdog. But I'm in no hurry. MacDara has a flight booked to New York three days from now. New York will do fine.* He swung the binoculars back in time to see MacDara rise to his feet and walk back towards Ardree House, picking his way through the hidden minefield of bogland swamp. He was beginning to enjoy his cat and mouse game with MacDara. Usually these contracts of Misha's were boring and predictable. Not this time. He was in no hurry to take out MacDara. He put the binoculars back in their case, slung them over his shoulder and began his trek back down to the main road.

MacDara was only six miles from Ardree House on a road that he had travelled numerous times. And yet he couldn't find the major's house. He turned back for the third time, traversing the same stretch of roadway. This time he saw it. The opening was barely visible between overgrown hedgerows and whin bushes. It had to be the entrance, he decided as the bushes brushed the side windows of his car. Once inside he could see that he was on a solid lane, much wider than he expected. It was covered with tufts of grass and weeds, testimony to its lack of use. A jungle of trees lined each side, blocking any vision of what lay beyond. So it was a surprise when he turned a corner to find himself in front of a house that had once been an elegant mansion. The architecture was mixed, part French chateau with Palladian style wings, but it had been allowed to deteriorate. An ornate fountain, now dry and surrounded by ferns and nettles, formed a centerpiece in the middle ground that used to be a circular driveway. As MacDara left his car and walked toward the front door he could imagine other days, days of dinner parties and carriages arriving with ladies and gentlemen in their finery.

MacDara was expected but not at the front door. A door in the right wing was ajar and Major Richard de Lacey, a tall thin, Patrician looking man in his early seventies, extended a bony hand with a remarkably firm grip.

"Mr. MacDara?"

"Please just call me Owen. And thank you for taking the time to see me."

"Do call me Richard. All the 'blow-ins' call me Major but the locals always refer to me as 'His Lordship' although I have never used that ridiculous title. And, Owen, don't thank me. Time is all I have these days. Now, just follow me. Mind your step here. The floor is a bit irregular at this corner."

They negotiated a narrow, dimly-lit corridor whose walls were covered with ancestral paintings, dark in pigment, many of them almost floor to ceiling, until they emerged into a flagstoned entrance hall squared between two enormous fireplaces. MacDara had a glimpse of pistols on the mantlepiece and crossed sabres on the wall as the Major's loping gait seemed to gather speed crossing the hall. Almost in a tour guide voice, without stopping or turning around, the Major said, over his shoulder:

"We haven't used this entrance in years. Not since our grandmother passed away."

Crossing into another corridor extending beyond the central entrance hall they soon reached a large dark green oak door. The Major opened it and ushered MacDara inside. The contrast was stark. Comfortable chairs, booklined walls, collectables and art, all warmed by a blazing fire in the hearth made the room personal, lived-in, human.

"Please make yourself comfortable," said the Major, directing Owen to a chair by the fire as he crossed the room to an array of drinks displayed on a corner table.

"Cognac, Irish, Scotch?"

" A Paddy please, if you have it."

"Indeed I do. I like it myself. Smooth. I'll join you."

The Major returned with two large Waterford tumblers generously filled with the amber glow of Irish whiskey. They toasted in the Gaelic.

"Slainte!"

The Major didn't sit down. Instead he wandered over to the bookshelves. He looked as though he intended to reach for a volume, then changed his mind and turned to face MacDara.

"The original De Lacey came to Ireland in the twelfth century with Strongbow. The Norman Invasion! And you know that Strongbow was Richard de Clare, the Earl of Pembroke, a Norman himself. So when the Irish say that the English invaded Ireland, it was really the Normans, my ancestors. A century or two later we'd become 'more Irish than the Irish themselves'. But you know all that, don't you,

Owen?"

"Yes, Richard," said Owen, and quickly tried to keep the Major from wandering, "the reason I came to see you..."

"I know the reason you came to see me," said the Major, and then proceeded as though that was unimportant. "How many of us own our ancestral lands today?" It was a rhetorical question. He didn't wait for an answer. "Very few. But we still do. It hasn't been easy. How much do you think it would cost to heat this whole place? The Colonial Service of the Crown. That's how we did it. That's how we kept our lands. We practiced the Art of War and the spoils of those foreign wars paid our servants and our debts. But the Empire ended and we weren't needed."

"And the Congo...?" MacDara tried again.

"What skills did I have? Only those of the warrior. It was either that or lose our lands. Can you see me in some one-roomed cottage? Of course you can't. So I fought for the person who paid me the most. Colonel Mike Hoare was a fellow Irishman. He and I had served together in the British army. So when he asked me to join him I couldn't refuse."

"But the CIA and MI5...and the KGB?" asked MacDara.

"Oh, don't be so naïve, Owen. I worked for all of them. Numerous times. War is a dirty business!"

"But why the Secretary General of the UN?" MacDara's tone got louder.

"The UN! Hah! They were not peacekeepers. They were up to their eyeballs in that mess in the Congo. The Secretary General was one of their Field Commanders. He was fair game and we weren't playing by the Marquis of Queensbury rules. Besides Colonel Mike could never have paid me what the Yanks and the Russians did. You see, Owen, I would have done anything to save our lands. I did not want to be remembered as the de Lacey who lost the ancestral home and sold off the family titles to some vulgar Texas oil millionaire."

He gulped down his whiskey, refilled his glass and offered Owen another. But Owen declined and went straight to the heart of the matter, his reason for being there.

"Richard, we know from the KGB documents that Zhukov was the Russian who contracted you for the Congo assignment but they didn't give the American's name. That's why I am here."

"You know, old boy, you really can't prove any of this and I've got little time left so it doesn't matter to me any more. Prostate cancer. Six months at best," said the Major matter of factly, as he finally conceded that his strength had ebbed and sank into the armchair opposite MacDara. Owen waited, sensing that he would get what he came for.

"I never liked the American. A bully, I'd say. It doesn't matter to me if you know his name or not. It was Kearns. Yes, that was it. I don't believe I ever knew his first name. We weren't really on a first name basis. But I don't see what good it will do you. It was obvious to me that they were just somebody's messenger boys. And you may not want to find out who that somebody was. For your own health, I mean."

The Major was enjoying the company and would have been quite happy to entertain MacDara all evening. But Owen had got what he came for and, as graciously as he could, made his exit. As he turned at the green oak door to say goodbye, the Major spoke again, his voice tinged with just the right sense of curiosity and bemusement.

"Owen, I do think you people should talk with

each other. I told all of this to that young Russian lady from the UN who came to see me a couple of days ago. What was her name? Nadia? Something like that."

Galway Airport

Owen MacDara walked out of the terminal building toward the waiting Fokker 50 turbo-jet. It looked new. He remembered the small propeller driven plane that he'd taken on his last trip from here. A very noisy plane that bounced around at the slightest turbulence in the air. He felt better about this flight.

He was first on board. A trickle of people followed and it looked like there was only going to be ten or twelve passengers. The last passenger climbed aboard just seconds before the stairs were pulled back. MacDara was surprised when the man chose to sit beside him seeing that there were plenty of empty seats in the plane.

"Hope you don't mind? I prefer company when I fly. But if I'm bothering you I'll be glad to move. Just say so."

"No, no, I don't mind. It's a short flight anyway," said Owen MacDara.

"Name's Conor Brady."

"Owen MacDara."

"Vacation over?"

"You could say that. But I keep a home here too. What brings you to Ireland?"

"Roots, I suppose. I was born here. County Mayo. But my family moved to Argentina when I was only five."

"I'm a Derryman. But I've spent most of my
life in the States. I'm sure that's pretty obvious."

"Oh, I don't know. There's still a bit of Ulster
in your voice. Where's your home?"

"Connemara.   I try to get back as often as I
can. To recharge the old batteries, you know."

"Connemara! That's a coincidence. I spent
the last few days there. In Clifden. Did a bit of
golfing, bit of fishing, a lot of drinking!"

"That's Clifden! Lives by its own rules."

The plane taxied out on to the runway and everyone
lapsed into the usual silence that descends at takeoffs
and landings. The acceleration was smooth and they
were in the air before they realized it. Conor Brady
exchanged   some   pleasantries   with   the   flight
attendant and turned to talk with Owen MacDara
again just as a loud noise, almost like an explosion,
rocked the plane. The plane dipped suddenly to the
right and the cups slid off the tray tables spewing hot
coffee and tea over everything.   Then the plane
seemed to commence a slow fall almost as though it
was coming in for a fast landing. MacDara's fists
clenched tightly on the handrests and he knew the
plane was going down.   A middle aged lady
diagonally across from him had taken out her rosary
beads and started praying in a loud voice:

"Holy Mary, Mother of God, pray for us
sinners now and at the hour of our death".

Conor   Brady   looked   across,   his   dark
complexion a shade grayer and said,

"It must be comforting to believe all that
stuff."

Just then the Captain's voice came over the
public   address   system.   He   sounded   steady,
controlled, but his words were not reassuring. He
explained that an engine had failed and there had

been damage to the controls. They were losing altitude and they would not be able to make the airport. He advised everyone to prepare for an emergency landing and said that he'd come back on the air just before landing. He then asked the flight attendant to prepare the passengers for an emergency landing. Owen looked around and saw the fear in people's eyes just before he crossed his arms, grabbed the back of the seat in front of him and rested his forehead on the back of his hands. He had no time to think about living or dying except for one crazy thought: *if I still believed like that lady I could look forward to seeing Kate again.* The last thing he heard before they crash landed was the Lord's Prayer from the woman with the rosary. The next sensation he experienced was the smell of jet fuel and somebody struggling to free him from the seat belt. He regained consciousness in the middle of a grassy green field and looked up at the face of Conor Brady as the plane exploded and flames and black smoke spiraled skyward.

ENDINGS

Pat Mullan

TRIBUNAL

TRIBUNAL was originally published in *Dublin Noir* (published by Akhashic Books in the US and by Brandon Books in Ireland and the UK). It is the *end of the beginning* of the novel *Last Days of The Tiger*.

ENDINGS   Pat Mullan

"All that is necessary for the triumph of evil is that good men do nothing "

Edmund Burke (1729-1797) Irish orator, philosopher, and politician.

ENDINGS   Pat Mullan

1

Dublin, 8:00 am

There's a buzz about the place. Sure as hell wasn't here when I left twenty years ago. He remembered Dublin as the pits then. Dark, priest-ridden, can't do culture, living on government handouts and money from the emigrants. A god-forsaken hole of a place. For himself anyway. Edmund Burke. *Yeah, that's me. My old man had delusions. Thought if he named me after the great Irish statesman that the name would overcome the bad genes and the lousy upbringing.* Willie Burke had been a failure, failed at every no-risk job he ever attempted, and the old man had ended his days earning a mere pittance as a salesman in a tailoring shop that had seen its best days in the last century. Mass on Sunday was the highlight of his mother's week, a timid woman from the west of Ireland who'd never felt 'at home in the big city. An only child, Edmund had been conceived as his mother's biological clock was about to stop ticking. She'd been forty-two when she had him.

All these things flooded his mind as he jumped into the taxi at Dublin airport and told the driver to take him to Ballsbridge. He'd survived. Succeeded because his father's failure terrified him. Got into Trinity, earned a law degree, headed for England, stayed a year in a boring clerk job in a London legal firm as resident Paddy. Luck intervened. His mother's uncle in Boston sponsored him to the States. Decided that he'd go by sea instead of air. Took a 28,000 ton liner out of Liverpool. Gave him a sense of being a pilgrim setting out for the New World.

Now he was back. Why? Money, that's why. Well, one of the reasons. He was running away again. But that's another story. Taking a year off from his New York law firm. Had about enough of his mob clients. As well as his ex who wanted to rob him blind. Oh yeah, he'd stashed away a few dollars but still hadn't made that million. Maybe Dublin's the place to be these days. Everybody's here. All these faces in Dublin on a Tuesday and you see them again in New York or L.A. at the weekend. Aidan Quinn. Gabriel Byrne. Liam Neeson. Colin Farrell. Michael Flatley now a household name with Riverdance conquering the world. And Michael O'Leary and Ryanair conquering the skies. The priests are scarce on the ground these days. Divorce is legal. The Bishop of Galway has a love child with an American lover and the President of Ireland has crossed the religious divide to take communion in a Protestant cathedral. The IRA is about to call it quits and the border separating the Republic from Northern Ireland is gradually becoming an imaginary line. Money talks. And money goes where it's well treated.

Money! That's really why I'm here, he reminded himself. *Not here to feel sentimental. Still, the old city looks good, he thought. New roads, new houses, construction cranes everywhere. Plenty of Mercs and BMWs. They're not taking the Liverpool boat anymore. No! They're in investment banking, working for McKinsey and Microsoft. Turning*

Ireland into the largest exporter of computer software outside of the United States.

At Ballsbridge Burke paid the taxi fare and walked up the Shelbourne Road. Dublin 4. The most sought after neighbourhood in Dublin. Bright skies and the early morning briskness countered his lack of sleep. Old stately homes lined the streets. Surrounded by sturdy stone walls, they exuded wealth and power. As a kid this would have been an alien place to him. *Still is*, he thought, as he reached a modern four-storey apartment block in Ballsbridge Gardens. He already had a key, mailed to him in New York before he'd left. Once inside, he realized that he could be anywhere. Luxury that would be right at home on Fifth Avenue. He dropped his bags, started the coffee machine, and minutes later sat in the large Jacuzzi bathtub watching the bubbles welcome him to Dublin.

2

Refreshed and dressed he arrived at Lillie's Bordello at six. The most elite club in Dublin. Had he been here a few nights ago, after the Irish Film and Television Awards, he could have joined Pierce Brosnan and James Nesbitt as they sang Danny Boy at the piano in the VIP room.

This was Murphy's idea. Drop him into the deep end. Meet who's who in Dublin society. Hit the ground running! That's always been Murphy's modus operandi. Murphy was his old law school buddy at Trinity and the reason he'd returned to Dublin. Murphy had built a successful legal business, rich from tribunal money and litigation. Now with more business than he could handle, he'd developed a distrust for his partners.

It didn't take much persuasion to tempt Ed Burke back to Dublin. His mob clients were a little annoyed at the moment. One with a bullet behind his ear in a ditch in Westchester. Another behind bars on a federal indictment for corruption.

Jesus Christ! I really could be in New York or LA! The same confidence. The same body movements. Damn it. Even the accents are mid-Atlantic. All the right people at tonight's reception for a noble cause. Charity. Aid for Africa. Medicine for Chernoble. Sexy stuff. Good publicity for the rich and powerful.

He felt a finger trace its way up his spine, lingered to enjoy, then turned slowly and came face to face with her.

"Edmund", she said, moving to within inches of him. The only person, other than his mother, who'd called him Edmund.

Just then Murphy arrived with drinks.

"Ah, a reunion, you two...OK! OK!" he protested their stares, handed Burke his drink, and moved on. But the spell had been broken.

"Pia, it's been a long time", said Ed, looking at the woman who had broken his heart. Days and nights of endless lovemaking when they both attended Trinity. Summers in Donegal. Running naked into the sea on the Fanad beach at midnight. Dark, Latin beauty, born in Barcelona, Irish father, Spanish mother. Something Irish flashing through, the same way you'd see the Irish in Anthony Quinn's Mexican face.

"Twenty years, Edmund. You're looking well. If I'd known you were going to be such a success ..." she let the sentence hang in the air as she thought he hadn't aged a day. Trim and erect at six feet with a classic Irish face, fair but tinged with a darker hue, probably from his west of Ireland mother. A few grey hairs only added lustre. And the confidence! *He was always so confident*, she thought, *I can imagine him in the courtroom.*

Ed wanted to hold her, kiss her, take her to that Fanad beach again. His mind spoke to him, *Oh Pia, I loved you so much. And you broke my heart when you left me for that geek, David Manning. Now he's the Minister for Trade and Industry and Tanaiste too, second only to the Taoiseach in the government. Being touted as a future Taoiseach. Speak of the devil.* The man himself approached. *Still the tall, lanky geek I remember. Wearing glasses now and the hair's thinning out.*

"Ed, I see you're back. Good. We need your talent here. Building a great country these days."

"Well, I'm looking forward to it, Tanaiste. Had things looked like this twenty years ago I might never have left."

"Well, you're back. That's what matters."

Looking at his wife, he said, "Pia, you and Ed are old friends. Introduce him around. New blood he should meet here."   And, with that, he was gone. Working the audience. Consolidating his mandate.

Pia and Ed's fixation was interrupted again by a tall, good looking, sandy haired man who said:

"Pia, aren't you going to introduce me?"

She turned around and looked into the eyes of Tom Flanagan. Tom, who had told her long ago if she couldn't return his love, then he'd be there for her as a friend and confidant at any time. He knew about Pia and Ed Burke and the past. Pia had told him all of that.

"Oh Tom, I didn't know you'd be here", she said, holding his hand between hers and kissing him warmly on the cheek.

"Tom, this is Ed Burke, an old friend. Just back from New York," and looking at Ed, "and Ed, this is Tom Flanagan, a very dear friend."

"Ed, good to meet you. Are you visiting?"

"No, Tom. I'm back. Giving Dublin another try. Who knows, maybe I'll stay this time. Are you the same Tom Flanagan that's giving Michael O'Leary a hard time these days?"

Flanagan's head went back in hearty laughter, "Oh, you've been reading the tabloids. They'd love to create a big drama out of all of this. O'Leary makes good headlines. Always shooting off his mouth. I don't see myself as a warm-up act for him."

"But *FlanAir* has grabbed a share of his market. That's sure to light a fire under him. You're warming him up alright!"

"Enough about me, Ed. What are you doing in Dublin?", knowing well that Burke was in the legal profession.

"I'm a lawyer. Joined the firm of an old law school friend. Plenty of tribunal business these days."

"Too much of it. But I suppose we're finally flushing the system of all the gombeen men and their brown paper bag handouts. This country has grown up and can no longer be run by people who use it to feather their own nests. The 'nod and wink' people have got to go. So good luck. Make sure you're defending the right people."

Then looking at Pia, he said, "I'm off to Brussels tomorrow. Probably be gone four or five days" and, leaning over, he kissed her and slipped a key into her hand.

"Good to meet you, Ed. I'm sure we'll be seeing more of each other. If you need anything, let me know."

Pia had the key to Tom Flanagan's apartment and they met there the next evening. A bottle of Armagnac, two crystal glasses, and a welcome note awaited them in front of the fireplace.

Ed Burke knew that it was a mistake. But he was addicted. Always had been. In the days that followed he and Pia threw caution to the wind. They were inseparable and indiscrete. Glued together in cosy corners in the best pubs and clubs, unabashedly naked in private saunas. It seemed their passion had only been fuelled by the passing of time.

3

Three weeks after his arrival Ed Burke found himself 'in at the deep end', defending Dan Mortimer, one of Dublin's elite, against a class action suit brought by a rabble of welfare dependent inner city denizens. As Murphy had said, " Good way to announce your presence to the world. This is a case you can't lose. And making an ally out of Mortimer will seal your career. Besides it'll be great PR for our firm." A good quarter of the construction cranes criss-crossing the Dublin skyline bore the Mortimer name in huge capital letters. The new dockland development had Mortimer stamped all over it.   But this case had aroused the emotions of the people. The class action suit claimed that Mortimer had illegally acquired derelict inner city land that should have been used for the community and had then used his influence to have it rezoned for commercial purposes. Site development had commenced, excessive noise polluted the air, cracks had appeared in the foundation of adjacent houses. The suit also claimed that Mortimer had used aggressive tactics to persuade local homeowners to sell and leave so that he could demolish their homes and make way for further commercial usage. Two hungry young lawyers represented the claimants. *Like me twenty years ago,* thought Burke, *idealistic and naïve.* They could not support their case with solid evidence. They promised to produce a witness who would testify that Mortimer had made illegal payments to someone in government to get the land rezoned. But the witness did not show up in court. The judge gave them a second chance. Produce the witness within one week. Otherwise the court finds the claim unsubstantiated.

A late evening wind blew the rain into Burke's face as he stood on the corner awaiting the taxi he'd ordered. It had been a long day in court and he felt uneasy about the whole business. New York was different. There he knew the good guys from the bad guys. Everything was direct. In your face. Here nothing resembled that. Too much grey, too little black and white. This country thrived on ambivalence.

An elderly man approached him. Something familiar searched his brain for a memory, a connection.

"Hello, Eddie."

The 'Eddie' completed the circuit in his brain. He hadn't been called Eddie since he was a little boy. Marty, Marty Rainey. Age now hid the vitality he remembered. Marty had been almost a surrogate father. Often there for him when his own father was down in the pub in the evening.

"Marty! Is it you?"

" 'Tis indeed. Not as supple as you remember. But the old head still works.""Marty, it's great seeing you again!"

"Eddie, I need to talk to you. It's life or death for me."

Saying it so matter-of-factly took the surprise out of it. The taxi pulled up, saving Ed from looking lost. He insisted on taking Marty home. As the taxi pulled out into rush hour traffic, Marty said:

"I'm your witness."

For a moment Ed Burke was mystified. Then it struck him that Marty's telling him that he's the missing witness at the trial. Ed gripped Marty's arm and looked at him. Marty continued:

"I couldn't show up. They threatened me. Told me that I'd wind up in the Liffey. They meant it, Eddie. I suppose I'm a coward."

"Who threatened you?"

"Thugs! That's who. You don't think they'd do their own dirty work, do you? No, they hired a bunch of thugs who don't give a shite. They'd kill me as easily as look at me."

"Who ordered it?"

"Come on, you know who. You're defending one of them in court. I suppose you're gettin' well paid for that. But you've forgotten where you came from, Eddie."

"Damn it Marty! Don't fucking lecture me! If you're telling me the truth, then you were the bagman for these bastards for years! Selling your own people down the drain!"

"You're right. I was stupid. Gambling, bookies, the horses. I owed too much and they paid it off. But, believe me, Eddie, I never thought they'd turn our own people out of their homes. I didn't know. Now I want to get them. The bastards. They destroyed me and I want to destroy them."

He reached inside his coat and pulled out a large bulky envelope.

"Everything's in here. All the evidence. Record of payoffs, who, where, and when. Bank account statements showing how the money was laundered. There's enough here to start a dozen tribunals. It'll destroy Mortimer and it'll bring down the Tanaiste. He's a corrupt bastard! The word around is that you're pretty close with his missus. Watch yourself!"

Ed Burke sat in silence holding the envelope as though it was a bomb. Which, in a sense, it was.

Before he could gather his thoughts, the taxi stopped outside Marty's front door in Harold's Cross.

Marty gripped his hand, said "Do the right thing, Eddie", and left.

And Ed Burke did the right thing. He met next day with Murphy and told him that he could not defend Mortimer, told him about Marty Rainey's evidence, told him that they'd have to meet with the judge and turn this evidence over to the court. Murphy reluctantly agreed and insisted that Burke secure the envelope with the firm for safekeeping until they could take it to court. Burke considered this to be sensible advice.

That evening, he waited until everyone had left the office. Then he copied every document in Marty's envelope. He replaced the originals with the copies and lodged the envelope in the firm's safe. He slid the originals into a new envelope and put it in his briefcase. Tomorrow he would take it to his safe deposit box at his bank. Burke did not trust the system. Anyone in the Attorney General's office could be a supporter of the Tanaiste. It would be easy for one or more incriminating documents to disappear. So he'd wait. When the evidence got that far and they needed the originals, he'd be glad to provide them.

4

Two nights later, the jarring ringing of his phone brought Ed Burke out of a deep slumber. He growled:

"Yeah?"

"Ed Burke? Is this Ed Burke?"

"What do you want? Do you know what time it is?"

"This is the emergency call service. We have an alert on Martin Rainey. We think he has fallen in his home and can't get up. He needs help. Can you go there now?"

"But I'm not on any alert system!"

"You're on it, Mr. Burke. Mr. Rainey insisted that we call you if he needed help."

Ed Burke decided that he had no choice. Marty Rainey wouldn't have put him on the alert list without a good reason. He confirmed Marty's address with the emergency service, dressed, and called a taxi.

At 3am with no traffic on the streets, the taxi reached Harold's Cross in fifteen minutes and dropped Burke at the end of Marty's street. A neat row of red brick houses wound in an arc ahead of him; houses that cost a few thousand only fifteen years ago now ran into hundreds of thousands. A cat scurried across the street in front of him, breaking the silence of the night.

He found number 27 and rang the doorbell. No answer. He rang it again, holding down the buzzer. Still no answer. Now he stood contemplating what he should do. He knew that he must get inside. Further down the street he saw a break in the pattern of the houses and what seemed to be a large commercial doorway. Counting the houses he reached it and got lucky. A smaller door stood closed but unlocked. He took out his flashlight, opened the door and passed through a dry stone wall, to find himself in an open grassy space at the rear of the houses. Counting back he reached Marty's house. The dry stone wall at the back provided a natural foothold. He climbed up. Marty's house, probably his kitchen, had been extended and took up the small backyard. Its flat roof backed up against the wall. Burke simply stepped onto it, reached up and leveraged himself onto a ledge outside the window on the second floor. His luck held. The window stood slightly ajar. He squeezed inside, shone his flashlight around, and saw that he stood on a landing at the head of the stairs.

Calling out Marty's name, he inched his way down the stairs to the living room. He found the light switch and turned it on. He saw the blood first. Pooled around Marty's head where he lay on his side in the middle of the room. A huge open gash crossed his forehead. Burke knelt down and took his pulse. No sign of life. He turned him over to try CPR and that's when he knew that this had been no accident. Marty's throat had been cut.

Burke waited till the ambulance and the Guards arrived and sealed off the house. As it was a crime scene, Marty would stay right where he lay until the State Pathologist arrived. The Guards took a statement from Burke and he left.

Burke made it back to his apartment by 4.30 AM. Too wired to sleep, he headed for the whiskey. Half a bottle later, he sank into a deep stupour.

5

Ed Burke arrived at the church as the requiem mass was beginning. Marty Rainey's coffin sat at the head of the centre aisle in front of the altar. Ed walked up the side aisle and took a seat midway up, near enough yet apart from the first three rows where Marty's close relatives were seated. *Close relatives, that's a joke,* thought Ed, *I'll bet none of them came to visit him when he was alive; now they're only here to be seen and maybe to hope that Marty left them some money...*

"Marty, I'm sorry," Ed said to himself, *"I shouldn't be thinking like this."*

Ed Burke reflected that he now only attended church for funerals and weddings. He found it hard to believe that heaven waited for the good and hell for the bad. On the plane over he'd been reading Richard Dawkins' *The GOD Delusion* and he thought that the quotation from Einstein described himself quite well: *I am a deeply religious non-believer.*

Ed's reflections were interrupted. People left their seats and started walking up the centre aisle towards the priest who was now waiting, at the foot of the altar, to administer the holy communion. He looked at the people as they returned to their seats, young, old, some threadbare, some in the best of clothes, all sombre and unsmiling in their attitude of reverence. And he felt lucky. Lucky to have escaped. The mass was over before he realized it. The four pallbearers lifted Marty's coffin onto their shoulders and carried it down the aisle to the waiting hearse outside. Marty's relatives followed and then the rest of the mourners. Ed waited at the edge of his pew as they passed. He didn't notice the red-eyed young man glance in recognition as he passed.

It rained, it poured unrelentlessly as they buried Marty. People stood in clusters under umbrellas at the graveside as the coffin was lowered into the grave and the priest recited the final prayers. Ed stood apart, in a raincoat with a hood over his head that permitted him a narrow vision of these last ceremonial moments. Nobody knew him here but he was here for Marty. That sufficed.

Suddenly it was over. A life was gone. The people huddled against the rain as they left. Ed turned and bumped into someone. He looked the person in the face and apologised. A young man, oddly familiar to him. It seemed that the young man knew him but didn't speak, just kept moving. And then it hit him. *Denis! Denis Rainey!* Marty's nephew. A kid of thirteen or fourteen when Ed had left Dublin for the States. Must be in his mid-thirties now. And Ed remembered the young boy who loved Marty, and Marty as the uncle who could relate to his autistic young nephew. That's it, remembered Ed, Denis suffered from an autistic spectrum disorder. He was an Asperger. In the minute or two that it took Ed to recall this, Denis had disappeared. Ed looked but couldn't find him.

A missed opportunity, he thought, *I would have really liked to talk to him.*

6

Pia! Pia! Ed Burke agonized about what to do. In days the scandal would break. The Tanaiste's career would crash. In public. And Pia would crash too. Every tabloid would exploit the story. Exploit her!

Thoughts bounced wildly around his head: *I've got to do something. Got to protect her. But how? I could leave again. Go back to the States. Take her with me. Start a new life with her. Agh, wishful thinking! It's too late for us. Pia won't leave Dublin. It's the centre of her world. All the world comes to Dublin now. So what's the incentive to leave? Why should I leave again? Got to brave this thing out.*

Still Pia must be warned. He must tell her what's coming. Get her to leave the Tanaiste. Get out first. Make the first move. Yes, that's what she must do. And he'd help her. Once he had decided, Burke took action. Called her mobile.She picked up immediately.

"Edmund, it's only nine AM"

"Pia,let's run away together. Now."

"Oh, Edmund. How I wish."

"Look, it's Friday. I'm off today. Let's go somewhere. Get away from it all. Can you break all your social commitments?"

"Yes! Yes! Yes!"

"OK, great! I'll make the arrangements. Pick you up by noon."

7

Too many days like this, thought David Manning, noting that it was ten after nine in the evening as his driver dropped him at the front gate of his home in Howth, *but it goes with the job.* Solar powered lights illuminated his way up to the front door. *Have to go green, take care of the environment, prevent global warming, set an example as Tanaiste.* Pia's constant harping about the environment invaded his consciousness. He turned the key in the door, entered the hallway and hung his coat in the cloakroom. An energy saving light in the chandelier that hung from the cathedral ceiling above shed just enough light to let him make his way through to the drawing room. Not a sound anywhere. No sign of his beautiful wife greeting him with cocktails and a huge kiss. The way it used to be in the beginning. Now she spent her days elsewhere. Usually in somebody's else's bed.

"Oh, Pia, where are you?" he yelled to no-one, *"Out screwing your old lover? Is that where you are? You and Burke in some cosy bolthole. Fucking each other's brains out, aren't you? Think I don't know. Or you don't give a shite. That's it, isn't it? Well, it's my house and my money, darling, and there'll be no divorce for you! Not a fucking penny, do you hear me?"*

He threw his jacket on the couch, left his briefcase on the coffee table, walked through to the bar and fixed himself a whiskey. Then he went out through the french doors to the deck where he sank into the cushions of one of the large deck chairs and looked out to sea.

Sipping his drink, he let his mind wander: Always wandering to my mother. Those little pictures in my head. Her laughter, her smell, her skin, her touch. Only five years old and I still remember. Waiting and waiting and waiting for her outside the shops. Said she'd be back in a minute. But she never came back. They said I'd been abandoned. But what did they know. Then the orphanage. A prison, a place of abuse and torture, run by a bunch of sadistic nuns and a priest who came around once a week to fondle me. How I hated it and hated them. The two years there seemed forever. Until the Mannings rescued me when I was seven. Hugh Manning, a farmer. Some farmer! Twenty acres of poor land in Roscommon, not enough to support them. So he worked as a labourer at every odd job he could find. And Mary, his wife, who couldn't have kids and couldn't find a baby to adopt. Hell no, all the unwed mothers' babies were given to the nuns to be shipped to places like Australia, never to be seen again. Sweep it under the carpet. No scandals in Holy Ireland! So Mary Manning settled for a seven year-old orphan. My son, she called me. And she promised that I wouldn't have to slave on a poor farm for a living. No, I would get an education. They scrimped and saved every penny so that, at eleven, she could send me off to boarding school.

"Damn!" Manning awoke from his reverie as the glass slipped out of his hand and hit the wooden deck at his feet, spilling the remaining half of his whiskey. He went back to the kitchen, got a fresh one, and returned. And started where he'd left off.

Boarding school! Another prison. Run by priests. Sadists worse than the nuns. Beat us all with leather straps, even if we simply ran across their precious lawn after a ball. Scraps for food while they dined on the best. But I promised myself that I'd show them. And I did, didn't I? Well, they haven't seen anything yet!

He shook himself out of his reverie, finished his drink, took his briefcase from the coffee table and walked down the hallway to his office. Might as well stay ahead of the game, he mused, as he took a sheaf of documents out of his briefcase and sat down at his desk to work on them.

The next evening Murphy met Tanaiste David Manning in Buswells Bar, where all the members of the Dail went for their regular tipple. Manning asked, "What'll it be, the usual?" and ordered two Jamesons with water chasers.

No preamble for Manning, he went right for the jugular, "If he brings me down, you go too"

Murphy said nothing.

"Did you hear me? You go too"

"Goddamit, he's my friend. Isn't there any other way. We could persuade him to lay off"

"Persuade, my ass! Do you realize he's been fucking Pia since he got back."

"I hate to say it but ..."

"Yeah, do you think I'm dumb? I know she's been screwing the world for the past five years. Well, it's over! She won't be making a fool of me any more"

"What do you mean?"

"Killing two birds with one stone. That's what I mean!"

"Jesus! You're crazy! I want no part of it."

"In for a penny, in for a pound! You knew that! Do you really want to lose the mansion in Howth, the little hideaway in Shady Lane in the Bahamas where you entertain your Caribbean beauties, your yacht and your membership in the Royal Cork ... Fuck no, you don't want to lose any of it. And you don't want a tribunal looking into everything while you rot your arse in Mountjoy !"

Murphy shut up and gulped down his Jameson. Just as quickly another, a double, appeared in front of him. He had to admit to himself that there was no way out. Ed Burke was an investment that he couldn't afford.

8

Burke chose well. *Get the hell out of Dublin,* the first command he issued to himself. *Go west young man,* said Horace Greeley in America. And that's what Burke did. Go west to Galway. He knew exactly where. *St. Cleran's.* Once the Galway home of film director John Huston. Been turned into a most exclusive guesthouse by another famous Irish American, Merv Griffin. Just the place for them, away from their Dublin 4 crowd. Time to tell Pia, time to hold her, time to decide.

After they'd checked in, Ed ordered a beer for himself and a cider for Pia. Looking around, he said, "John Huston must have loved this place. I think Angelica lived here when she was a little girl."

Ed had always been a movie fanatic. When he was eleven or twelve, he used to save every penny to pay for his weekly trip to the cinema. Always American movies.

"Ah, so getting me out here was a ruse. You only wanted to spend the weekend in John Huston's home!"

Ed smiled, reached across and held her hand.

"What's the matter? There's something wrong, isn't there?"

"Yes, I'm afraid so. That's really the reason I brought you here. Get you away from Dublin right now."

Pia squeezed Ed's hand, encouraging him to continue.

"You know I've been defending a very close friend of your husband's in this Barton Tribunal.

Mortimer, the developer. Defending him against charges that he had property rezoned for his own commercial use, evicting people from their homes, among other things. There were charges that he paid off ministers in this government to have the land rezoned. Charges levelled right at the Tanaiste. It's his ministry and under his watch. But no-one could get any evidence to help them make any of these charges stick. Until an old friend of mine showed up one evening."

Ed finished his beer and Pia said, "You never told me any of this. Of course I never really asked you what you were doing. I've been so happy being with you these last few weeks."

"Pia, I know. But I have to tell you now. That's why we're here. That old friend *was* Marty Rainey. He was murdered a few days ago!"

"Oh, my god! How? Why?"

"I've jumped ahead of myself. Marty was supposed to be a witness at the tribunal. A witness against Mortimer. But he'd been threatened and had been afraid to turn up. He had a lot of important documents. Pretty incriminating against Mortimer. And others. Maybe even the Tanaiste."

"What happened to the documents?"

"I have them. Put them in the company safe. Murphy'll turn them over to the tribunal."

"But Marty ..."

"I found his body. In his own home. His throat had been cut. It wasn't any robbery or random act of violence. Believe me. It was an execution. I believe whoever did it was looking for Marty's documents. This will all hit the papers in the next couple of days."

"And you think that David ..."

"I don't think it! I'm sure of it. This will point a finger directly at him. He's going to be in a hot seat.

And you'll be there with him. That's why I wanted to get you out of there. Get you away before this all blows up in your face."

"I wish I could stay away."

"Listen, Pia, it's your choice to make, you know that, don't you? You know what I feel about it."

They talked about the scandal that would break in the days ahead and teased out all their options, all their choices. And Pia agreed to leave the Tanaiste as soon as they returned to Dublin. Brave out the turbulence ahead. They retired early, Pia reminding him that they had run away together.

Much later they noticed the bottle of Chablis, sitting invitingly in a crystal cooler. Into their second glass, Ed began to feel drowsy, a drugged feeling, and saw that Pia had already closed her eyes and had sunk into the pillow beside him. Moments later, he followed her.

9

Ed Burke's eyes hurt. Bad. His head hurt too. Worse. He tried to open his eyes. Couldn't. Sunlight grilled him through the open blinds. Eyes closed, fighting to stay awake, he slid out of bed, stood up, and felt his way to the window. Gripping the curtains, he yanked them closed and then risked opening his eyes. They still hurt but he could see. Turning around, he stopped, halfway between the window and the bed. Pia lay there, naked, one leg dangling on the floor, a trickle of blood from her lips forming a small red pond between her breasts.

Shocked, he stood impaled to the floor. His head throbbed and his heart thumped. He moved, unsteadily, towards the bed and knelt down beside her. Her right arm hung over the edge of the bed. He reached for it, tenderly, knowing that the life had left her. Yet he still felt for a pulse, hoping against hope.

Finally he released her wrist and sank onto the floor. His anguish seemed too much to bear. He rolled over into a foetal position and squeezed his head between his arms, wrapping his hands over his ears, shutting out the world, shutting out the reality that Pia was dead. He howled like a wounded animal. Then the tears came, an unstoppable flow. He suppressed the sounds of his own crying until it became impossible and he cried loudly and inconsolably.

He blamed himself for taking Pia away, to this safe place where they killed her. His infatuation had turned to love in recent days and he had hoped that there might have been a future for them. Now, in the darkness of his soul, he didn't even see a future for himself.

He stayed that way for a long time. Until the shock and sorrow turned to anger. Until his mind emerged from its drugged state.

Drugged! We were drugged! The wine! And they murdered Pia. They're making it look like I killed her. They? No fucking they! Only one person did this, only one person responsible! Manning! I'll get him if it's the last thing I do! I'll get him!

Anger dragged him out of his stupour. Rising to his knees, he gripped the bedside table and pushed himself back on his feet.

Then he reached for the phone.

ENDINGS   Pat Mullan

The Last Blow

The Last Blow is an extract from *Last Days of The Tiger* – edited out and left on the 'cutting room floor', not because it was bad. Because it did not fit the story. You don't need to read the novel to get a sense of the story. There's enough here to give you the backstory and let you see where this slice fits. It is an ending after all – the violent ending of the lives of two old friends. The brutality that fills our news headlines every day.

ENDINGS   Pat Mullan

The Last Blow

Dublin

Bob McArdle was Marty Rainey's closest friend, perhaps his only friend. About the same age and similarly saddled with life's infirmities, they met about once a week to bemoan the brave New Ireland. They usually met for lunch, fish and chips for both of them, and then, if the weather was dry, they'd sit near the canal not far from Portobello Road and watch the swans.

Today they sat silently looking at the swans until Marty said, "Bob, will you do something for me?"

Bob looked at him very strangely, "That's a strange question. If I can do it, I'll do it. You know that. Unless it's a bank job. Can't run as fast anymore!" And then chuckled at his own sense of humour.

"I want you to keep something for me."

"Sure, what is it."

Marty pulled a large envelope out of his pocket. He held it in his hand as he looked at Bob.

"There's a tape in here. It's a recording of a phone call. I want you to look after it for me. And, if anything happens to me, I want you to give this to the right person."

"Does this have anything to do with all that tribunal business?"

"It does. But it's even bigger than that. And there are some people who would like to get their hands on what's on the tape. That's' if they knew I had it."

"Marty, are you in any kind of trouble?"

"I'll be honest with you, I am. That's why I'm giving you this to keep for me."

"You need protection. Are you talkin' to the gardai?"

"They're the last people I'd be talkin' to. Can't trust anybody."

"But you said I should give this to the right person if anything happens to you. How will I know the right person?"

"That's where I'm relyin' on you. Don't give it to the police or the tribunal or anybody in the government."

"That's everybody!"

"No, you have to find someone you can trust. Somebody who's not afraid to go public with this tape, get it in the papers, on the TV, whatever. Somebody who's not afraid of them."

"I dunno, Marty. I just dunno. You can't let anything happen to you. Do ye hear me, do ye?"

Marty put his big arm around Bob and gave him a hug. Then he slipped the envelope into his hand, got up and walked away.

That was the last time that Bob McArdle would ever see Marty Rainey. Marty was found next day lying face-down on his kitchen floor The door keys were still in his right hand. His throat had been cut. A professional job.

At thirty-four Sean White had buried his father and moved back into the family home to take care of his sixty-five year old mother in the early stages of Alzheimers.

Married at nineteen, separated at twenty-one, and divorced in 2003 when Ireland finally made divorce legal. Sean had led a hedonist lifestyle for the past ten years. Gifted with boundless energy, his big open face acted as a magnet for many young ladies. But as soon as any relationship turned serious, Sean moved on. He feared commitment, fearing failure itself. But his lifestyle had worn thin in the past three years and had turned into too many hung-over mornings that were beginning to affect his career. A top investigative journalist, he'd been threatened often. He hadn't made the front page in a long time. Only his talent had saved him but he knew that that wouldn't last. So, in a sense, his father's death and the need to care for his mother saved him.

It was eleven on Saturday morning and he was in the kitchen preparing tea and toast for his mother when he heard the phone ring. She answered it and he could tell from her voice and her questions that she felt uncomfortable.

Probably another damn sales call, he thought.

He walked through to the hallway and found his mother standing there with the phone in her hand, looking bewildered, "I don't know who this is. But he says he wants to speak to you, Sean."

Sean took the phone from his mother and said, "Hello."

Spluttering coughs came over the line, followed by, "Is this Sean White?"

"Yes, who's speaking?"

More coughing, then, "I'm a friend of Marty Rainey."

Taken aback, Sean said nothing.

The man sounded elderly and unwell as he continued, "Marty was my closest friend. He gave me something before he died."

Sean asked, "What's your name?"

"Never mind that. I'll tell you when we meet."

"Why are you calling me/"

"I didn't know what to do or who to call. Marty didn't trust anybody. Not even the gardai. He gave me an envelope. Told me, if he died, to give it to the right person. I asked him who. But he said he'd trust me to find the right person."

"And why me?"

"I've seen your name on all the stories about Marty. About the documents too. Marty's documents. I know that. They killed him for them, didn't they?"

"Yes, they did!"

"Well, I want you to have whatever's in this envelope Marty gave me."

"Where do you want to meet?"

"I live near Marty. Harold's Cross. Meet me at *Peggy Kelly's*. Nine tonight."

"OK, I'll be there. And I want to bring somebody with me."

"Who?"

"Dave Smith. He's a trusted colleague. And it pays to be careful, doesn't it?"

The incessant coughing and spluttering had returned, finally followed by a wheezing, "Alright."

Bob McArdle left his house at eight and crossed the canal near the house where the Irish patriot, Robert Emmett, had been arrested. Aided by a strong blackthorn walking stick, he gritted his teeth against the pain of his sciatic nerve as it flowed through his right hip and down his thigh. But, at eighty-three, he'd learned to live with pain. Propelling himself on his blackthorn, he intended to be at *Peggy Kelly's* by nine.

Sean White and Dave Smith walked through the door of *Peggy Kelly's* at exactly eight-thirty. A big, bustling, neighbourhood pub, it was filled with people, young and old, eating, drinking, talking, laughing, enjoying. An infectious atmosphere.

Taking a pint of Guinness and a pint of Carlsberg from the bar, they squeezed their way through and found stools at a small round table in the rear.

"If you don't know who he is, Sean, do you at least know what he looks like?"

"No. But he knows what I look like and he said he'll find me. So we'll have to depend on that."

Dave raised his beer and clinked Sean's Guinness with a "Slainte!"

Taking a long, satisfying sip of his Guinness, Sean looked at Dave and said, "I think this whole Tribunal business is only scratching the surface."

"What do you mean?"

"Come on, they're getting nowhere. You know that. You could fill a library with the testimony they've taken."

"Do you know a better way?"

"There's got to be. It's costing the taxpayer a fortune. And making more fecking millionaires out of the lawyers!"

"Look at the big picture. We have to stop the culture of corruption. End the days of the gombeen man. This is a modern democracy and the old ways have to go. You could view these tribunals as an indictment of the past and a bridge to the future."

"I'll let the historians tell us that when they look back at this time. Maybe you'll be right. But I wouldn't bet on it. We're floating in money. And that's too much temptation."

"I know, I know. But, dammit, we need to send a message to these people! And to the countries and businesses that invest and trade with us. That we are honest and can be trusted. Right now they're waiting to hear from us. And the tribunals are a message to them as well."

"Ok, Ok. But I still say we're spending a ton of money on these tribunals. And for what? Have we arrested anybody? Jailed anybody?"

"No, not yet. Have faith. Look at it from another angle. We've exposed some of these people. Left them with tarnished images. They'll never run for political office again. They'll never hold positions of trust in this country again. Let's face it, they're finished!"

"That's too soft a landing for some of these bastards. They should be in Mountjoy, on bread and water, for the next twenty years!"

"You're right. And if the Tribunal finds enough hard evidence they'll be happy to turn it over to the DPP."

"I wish I could believe that."

"Damn it, you know we're not going to depend on the Tribunal to stop them!"

"I'm sorry. I get so pessimistic at times."

They both realized that they had got so caught up in their conversation that they'd forgotten entirely about the reason they were there.

"It's 9:15 already."

"Shit, I almost forgot."

"No sign of anybody yet."

"No. But he sounded old. And sickly. So I'm not surprised he's late."

Sean took their two empty glasses up to the bartender and said, "*Agus aris!*"

A light drizzle obscured Bob McArdle's glasses. Couples scurried past him and a stray dog almost tripped him. Distracted, he didn't see the two balaclava hooded men step out of a doorway as he hobbled along. One kicked the blackthorn stick out of his hand while the other kicked him in the ribs as he fell. He screamed in pain but the sounds died in his throat as the first assailant wielded the blackthorn like a baseball bat, cracking McArdle's cheekbone and forcing his broken dentures down his throat, blocking his windpipe. Swinging the blackthorn again, he smashed it into McArdle's back before tossing it on the ground. Dying now, his blood merging into the rain and running in rivulets into the drain near his head, the last blow of the blackthorn was unnecessary. The few people who saw the assault fled to the other side of the street. Assuming it to be another gangland killing, they knew it didn't pay to interfere or to even be seen. As the two assailants disappeared, another man, tall and sinister in a long *Jack Murphy* raincoat, stepped out from the shadows and kneeled at Bob McArdle's side. He fished an envelope out of McArdle's pocket. Then he stood and disappeared into the shadows.

At 10:30 Sean White and Dave Smith decided to call it an evening. They speculated that their appointee may have been too ill to show up. They reckoned that, if the caller had been real, they could only hope that he'd call Sean again.

Neither of them connected this with the news item in the next day's paper about the brutal bludgeoning death of a frail old man three streets away from *Peggy Kelly's*.

The AVENGER

The AVENGER evolved into the novel, *Creatures of Habit,* which is now available on-line as an ebook and as a paperback. If you'd like to see what happens to '*The AVENGER*' do read *Creatures of Habit.*

ENDINGS   Pat Mullan

1

St. Curnan's, Ireland

The two boys, breathless, reached the west corner of
the big study hall and flattened themselves against
the granite wall. Night had fallen and the wind had
reached gale force. Sleety rain sliced the air like
sheets of broken glass. The trees bent and groaned.
Wearing short trousers, their legs were scorched red
from knees to ankles.

They could see the flashlight coming towards
them and they knew they'd have to run again. So
they left the shelter of the wall and dashed past the
handball   court   as   the   lightning   illuminated
everything. Exposed, they cut across the front lawn
and ran towards the outer wall. They could hear the
loud squelch of running feet behind them.

A line of ancient oak trees stood like sentries
inside the outer wall. They hid between the trees,
hoping their pursuers would pass them by. But that
was a false hope. The flashlight reached the trees,
weaving in and out, getting closer and closer.
Panicked, Patrick, the older boy, started to climb the
nearest tree. Terry, the younger boy, tried to follow
but couldn't. So he ran, blindly, out of the shelter of
the trees. Patrick sat on a branch as the flashlight
passed beneath him. He had stopped breathing and
his heart thumped so loudly he imagined they must
hear it. But they moved on, following Terry as he
fled.

Now alone and terrified, Terry ran into the blinding rain, his lungs seared from the effort. Lightning flashed again, silhouetting the old ruined tower that stood inside the north-east boundary of the school. He stumbled over the uneven lumpy ground and, as the lightning flashed again, he saw the scaffolding clinging to the side of the tower. Erected recently by workmen hired to halt the deterioration, it seemed to offer him hope. Reaching the bottom of the scaffolding, he saw a wooden ladder the workmen used to get up to the first level. He started to climb as the lightning ended and the tower once again became pitch-black like the night above. On the first level he crawled over the rough wooden planks that bridged the gap between the metal scaffolding rods until he could feel the tower wall. Standing up he grabbed the next horizontal rod and, bracing himself between it and the wall, leveraged himself to the top level. Now he could hear voices nearby and streaks of light from a flashlight threw ribbons of white across the scaffolding. Trapped now, he realized he had nowhere to go. If he went back down he knew they'd get him. Backing up he found himself on a ledge near the door. He squeezed into the door frame, hoping to somehow disappear.

"We've got him! He's in the tower!" The first priest with the flashlight looked back at his companion, triumph in his voice.

"There he is!" he cried, shining his flashlight upwards until the boy stood transfixed in the glare, like a rabbit caught in a car's headlights.

"Don't! Take the light off his eyes!" The second priest, cautious, held the first priest's arm, "Let me talk to him."

The first priest hesitated and then moved the light away from the boy's face, "All right, we'll try it your way."

"Terry, can you hear me?

No answer.

The boy stood, fixed like a gargoyle, urine dripping down his bare legs and running into his socks.

"Terry, we are not going to hurt you. We only want you to give us your camera phone. The one you took the photos with."

No answer.

"Terry, you know we can't let you keep the photos, don't you?"

No answer.

"Terry, give us the phone and we'll say no more about it. Don't you want to go back to your room? You could catch your death out here on a night like this. You don't want to die over a few photos, do you Terry?"

No answer.

The first priest, '*I told you so'* in his tone of voice, cut in, "OK, we tried it your way. It didn't work, did it? Now we'll do it my way."

With the flashlight carving a path ahead of him, he moved to the foot of the ladder and started to climb. The boy saw him coming but he was cornered, nowhere to go. The priest, agile and sure footed, soon reached the top level of scaffolding, within easy reach of the boy.

"Give it to me! Now!"

The boy squeezed even further into the door opening. Sobs gurgled somewhere deep in his throat.

The priest, patience exhausted, reached for the boy. But the boy, terrified, tried to squeeze further into the door, lost his balance and fell.

113

Seconds later, they heard the thump of his body on the rocks below.

"Oh, dear God, he's dead!" The words, almost a wail, escaped from the second priest as they stood over the boy's body.

The first priest took the boy's pulse and said, "Yes, he's dead." He knelt down beside the boy and searched the pockets of his school blazer. Then he searched the pockets of his trousers.

"Nothing!"

"Maybe he lost it somewhere tonight. Or maybe it's lying around here. Could have fallen out of his pocket."

They started to search, lighting arcs around the body, guessing how far away from the tower a phone could have landed. After fifteen minutes they abandoned the search.

"What will we do about him?" asked the second priest.

"Nothing! Leave him here! When he's missing tomorrow, the prefects will search for him. Someone will find him."

"There'll be an investigation."

"No, there will be no investigation. It's an accident. Another dare gone wrong. Climbing the tower on a stormy night."

The second priest couldn't disagree. He knew that some of the boys got up to daredevil antics, climbing the walls after lights out, things like that. But Terry was never one of them.

"What will we do about the phone? What if it's lost and somebody finds it?"

"I don't think he lost the phone. He hid it. Or he gave it to someone."

They had almost reached the priests' residence hall and the storm had abated. The first priest stopped, turned to the second and said, with conviction: "That's it! He gave the phone to someone. We followed two of them tonight. And we lost one of them. Who was he?"

"We don't know."

"Well, who was young Terry friendly with? Who was he close to? "

"That's it, he wasn't close to anyone. He was quiet. A loner. Kept to himself. I tried to get him to participate. But he always held back, stayed on the fringes."

"Well, he must have a friend somewhere. He wasn't alone out there tonight. We've got to find that other boy. Soon!"

2

Monsignor Thomas Fallon, President Emeritus of St. Curnan's, still retained an office and a position as faculty advisor at the school. Now seventy-three, his power and influence remained undiminished. A lesser man would have been moved to one of the Church's retirement homes to spend the rest of his days in anonymity. But not Monsignor Fallon, who was politically connected all the way to the College of Cardinals in Rome. Plump and effete in manner, he sat in utter disbelief as Father Roland Cormack finished talking.

"Roland, this is a disaster!"

"I know! I wish I could turn the clock back."

"They'll say that you killed this boy!"

"But I didn't. He fell. It was an accident."

"Listen to yourself. If it's discovered that you followed this boy up into that tower and caused his death, they'll charge you. Murder or manslaughter, what's the difference? It'll be a show trial. They're out to get us now. Here, in the US, everywhere! This is a disaster!"

"No, no! There's nothing to suggest I was there when the boy fell. Only Father Nugent knows. And he won't say anything."

"How can you be so sure?"

"He's a wimp! You know him. He wouldn't say 'boo to a fly'."

"And why was he out there with you if he's such a wimp?"

"He knew about the photos. He thought he could talk to Terry. Get the phone from him. He liked the boy and he wanted to protect him."

"Father Nugent knows too much, that's what I think. And I think he's a risk."

"No, our big risk is that phone. The photos. We don't know what Terry Joyce did with it, or who he might have given it to."

"It's *your* big risk, not *our* big risk. Find that phone. Search everywhere. Find the boy who was with him last night."

"And if I don't find the phone?"

"Well, then you'd better hope it's lost, buried somewhere forever!"

After Father Cormack had left, Monsignor Fallon sat for a long time in contemplation. Then he picked up the phone and called Rome.

Next day Roland Cormack departed Dublin Airport on *Alitalia Flight AZ 3581*_at 2:15 pm. With a stopover in Paris, he arrived at Leonardo Da Vinci Airport in Rome at 9 pm, fifteen minutes late. Craving privacy, he avoided the express train and took one of the white cabs instead. Cardinal Volpe was expecting him at the Vatican

3

Even at sixty, Father Bernard Flaherty, the Irish teacher, was athletic and virile with the body of a man twenty years younger. While others read their morning breviary in their rooms, he donned a pair of sneakers and read his as he fast walked around the perimeter of the college grounds.

The light morning mist began to lift as he reached the stand of oak trees. He lifted his head to enjoy the beginning of a new day. But the sight ahead brought him to a sudden stop.

He stood, transfixed, clenching his breviary until his knuckles started to hurt. Shaking himself, he took the final few steps until he stood directly under the body that hung from the tree: a boy in the school blazer, short grey trousers, socks, no shoes. His neck twisted grotesquely out of the make-shift noose and his swollen tongue protruded from his mouth, gobs of saliva and mucous forming a trail down the front of his blazer.

Father Flaherty blessed himself and sank to his knees. He couldn't reach the boy so he recited the Act of Contrition where he knelt and asked God for forgiveness.

Then he got up, turned and ran towards the College.

He bounded through the front door, almost colliding with a group of students emerging from their breakfast in the refectory. He took the stairs two at a time, catching President McCafferty as he was about to enter his office. Sliding to a halt, he startled the President who turned around to see a red-faced Father Flaherty gasping for breath with sweat trickling down his cheeks.

"Father, what's wrong?"

"It's terrible, the boy ... he's dead!"

"Come in, come in ..." President McCafferty, now alarmed, gripped Father Flaherty by the arm, pulled him inside the office, and closed the door.

"What're you talking about? Who's dead?"

"Patrick Carty. He's hanging – from that tree – look out your window!"

Father Flaherty had gained control again. His face was still red but now from anger. He steered the President to the large office window the overlooked the front portico and commanded a view of the lawns that swept down to the main gate and the line of oak trees, now majestic in the morning sun.

"He's hanging from that tree!   And we're responsible. We took that boy's life."

President McCafferty stood transfixed before the window. He couldn't see the boy. His eyes were blurry with emotion. Somewhere deep inside he managed to get a grip on himself and turned to face Father Flaherty.

"Bernard, I'm as shocked as you. But I reject your accusation that we're to blame." With that, he strode to his desk, sat down and pulled the phone towards him.

But Father Bernard Flaherty would not be dissuaded, "I warned you! I knew this would happen. First that Joyce boy, now young Carty. Somebody has to pay. We have to take responsibility for this!"

"Bernard, Bernard, I've listened to you rant and rave like this so many times. You've alienated most of our faculty with your wild accusations."

"Wild accusations! Have you not been reading the newspapers? People have spat on me as I walked down the street. Spat on me! Do you hear me? Me, a priest, and they spat on me! I warned all of you that we must do something about this. Now it's too late!"

"Father Bernard, you're not helping. I do not want you charging around the school like this. Go to your room and pray for the soul of this unfortunate boy. I'm going to call the Gardai now. Then I'm going to call an assembly. I want the faculty and the students to hear this news from me. And I want the impact contained. Contained! Do you understand?"

But Father Bernard Flaherty was already on his way out, banging the large oak door behind him as he left.

A different Father Bernard Flaherty emerged from President McCafferty's office. He was no longer the light-hearted person who'd been out for his morning run. With the loose easy-going stride gone, the body had stiffened, the arms swung threateningly, the gait now one of an automaton, even the open face now closed into a bleak impenetrable visage. His hair, naturally tousled, sleeked back with sweat, now seemed designed for more serious purpose.

Once inside his own room, he put down his breviary and went to his bureau, pulled out the top drawer, retrieved a bottle of pills prescribed to him and clearly marked *prozac*. He opened the bottle and tipped one into the palm of his hand. Then he reached into the drawer again and squeezed two paracetamol tablets from a sheet of tinfoil. At the sink, he filled a glass with water and washed all three down his throat.

He sat down on the floor, in the lotus position, and started to chant in Latin ...

At twelve noon exactly Father Bernard Flaherty stepped onto the handball court. A tall three-sided concrete built court, it served as a whipping boy for him. On evenings and weekends, when he wasn't jogging, he was on the court, usually with an attentive, hypnotized audience. Boys would silently line both sides of the court, hands in pockets, watching every move he made, every time his hand whacked the ball with definite malice up against that wall. Every time he hit the ball, the boys' hands would strike in unison, punching inside the pockets of their trousers. This action was called *hinching*. Seemingly unaware of their involuntary complicity they would stand transfixed until he finished, *hinching* every time he struck the ball. But today he had no audience. He held the ball firmly in his hand, bounced it off the ground, and struck it hard with his right hand.

He kept this up until he collapsed, red-faced and breathless.

4

His foot slipped but he hung on. Suspended twenty feet above the ground, he hung on to a small tree that grew stubbornly out of the rock fissure. Winded, with muscles that hurt, sheer willpower and revenge drove him on.   Finding sounder footing, he rested and looked around.

Everything looked ghostly in the dusk.   The lights of the town glimmered in the distance. Looking up, he could see the top of the college walls five or six feet above his head.   He started to climb again.

Almost there.

The luminous dial of his watch read 10 pm.   Stars decorated the sky above. He sat in a sheltered cove behind the wall. He'd been here for over an hour. When he reached here, there'd been enough light left to show the hundreds of cigarette butts that now carpeted the ground beneath his feet.   Students' secret smoke hole.   Well hidden but holding a good view of the college and its grounds,   perfect for keeping a look-out for the prefects or even the Dean.

Clothed totally in black, he wore a black ski cap that could easily convert to a balaclava.   A rope hung, lariat style, over his left shoulder.

It's time, he said to himself.

The school grounds were deserted. All the students were now in their dorm rooms, in bed with the lights out. Four or five windows shone like beacons on the second floor of the faculty residence hall. One light shone out of the large French windows overlooking the roof of the main building's entrance porch. The President's office.

Rested after his climb, he ran across the sloping front lawn until he reached the shelter of the main building. Out of breath, he stopped for a minute and then moved cautiously, close to the building, until he reached the entrance porch.

Taking the rope from his shoulder, he threw it up and lassoed one of the marble stanchions mounted on top of the porch. He hooked the end to his belt and rappelled himself to the roof of the porch. Light from the French windows suffused out in a circle, leaving the edges of the porch in darkness. He looped the rope around the stanchion and, carrying one end, crawled across the porch to the edge of the French doors. Slightly ajar to let in some fresh air, he could see President McCafferty sitting erect at his desk, reading from a stack of papers. In his late sixties, his bald held alleviated by clumps of white hair at his temples, his ruddy face testimony to the outdoor athletic life he had led as a young man, as a star of the local Gaelic football club, he seemed preoccupied and totally unaware that he was about to have a visitor.

Vengeance is mine. Good enough for the Lord, good enough for me.

President Sam McCafferty dropped his papers and stood up in shock. The black clad man had entered his office through the French windows and was now

123

standing holding the end of a rope. He said nothing, just stood there, fully intent on unnerving him. President McCaffrey thought fast. Too late to call anyone to help. Besides they didn't live in a high risk place so they had never felt the need for their own security force. *No, I'm on my own, he thought, I'll have to talk my way through this.*

"Who are you?"

No answer.

"What do you want?"

No answer.

"I have no money or valuables here. If you've come to rob me, you've wasted your time."

No answer.

"If you talk to me, maybe I can help you."

No answer. The man took a couple of steps into the office and looked around, as though searching for something.

"Won't you tell me what you want? Maybe I can help you."

No answer.

President McCaffrey realized he was getting nowhere and wondered if he could make a run for it. If he could move out from behind his desk and edge his way towards the door, maybe he could do it. So he came out from behind his desk and stood to the side, saying,

"If you're in some kind of trouble, maybe I can help you. You can talk to me."

No answer.

The man's eyes seemed angry. The rest of his face was covered in a black balaclava.

"I won't tell anybody. No need to involve the police. Whatever trouble you're in, you need to talk to someone."

No answer.

The President decided to take the first step towards the door. But, as he did so, the man took some things out of his pocket and threw them at him. They hit his chest and dropped on the floor at his feet.

"Pick them up!"

The voice, loud and angry, showed no sign of weakness. The President found himself thrown off-balance, his plan of escape unattainable. Nothing to do but obey, play this thing out, and hope for the best.

He bent down and picked up the items from the floor. Students' caps with the school emblems pinned on the front.

"Look inside. Read the names!"

President McCaffrey read the names and his ruddy face suddenly lost all its colour. Now he knew the visitor's purpose. His legs started to tremble,

Fuelled by fear, the President made a dash for the door. Too late. The man rushed him, grabbed his soutane so fiercely that it ripped from the neck to the waist. The President had never been a fighter and had lived a life of non-violence, but now he kicked out at his assailant and landed a blow to the man's thigh. Which only infuriated the man who swung his fist and connected with the President's jaw, stunning him and knocking him to the ground. Vulnerable now, the President could feel the rope around his neck and hear the man's voice, a voice vaguely familiar.

"An eye for an eye. A tooth for a tooth. Isn't that what the bible says? Well, isn't it? A life for a life!"

The man tightened the noose around the President's neck and, with almost superhuman strength, began to drag him across the floor towards the French windows. The President tried to dig his heels in, tried to resist, but the man tightened the noose.   Once out through the French windows, the man grabbed the other end of the rope, already looped around the stanchion, and commenced to tug, just like a tug-of-war game. The President, unable to resist, slid inexorably towards the edge of the roof. Finally the man kicked him over the edge and braced himself as the President's body jerked the rope taut.

Vengeance is mine. Good enough for the Lord, good enough for me.

5

An angry Monsignor Thomas Fallon bounded down the stairs of St. Curnan's, rushed out the front door, and headed for his car. In twenty minutes he was on the main road heading west. Checked the clock on the dashboard: almost four thirty. He turned on the radio. Music wasn't his thing, certainly not the pop tunes that filled the airwaves from Radio2. Then he realized that *The Last Word* talk-show was about to start on TodayFM. *That'll do nicely,* he thought, *help to kill the next hour or so.* Leaning over to turn on the radio, the car behind annoyed him. Even though it wasn't dark, its headlights were on full. Maybe he'll turn off and I'll lose him soon. Cautioning himself to relax, he turned up the volume and drove at a steady sixty miles an hour.

The Avenger had been waiting for this opportunity for days. The monsignor was evil. He knew that. And no-one had done anything about it. Now the monsignor had covered up a crime and moved the guilty one out of the country. Moved him to Rome where he'd get protection. The Church had failed. Failed to purge itself of this evil. The Church had lost its way. These evil people were no better than the Templars who used to reject Christ and spit on the cross. But God found a way to make them pay. We burned them at the stake. Well, I am doing God's work. I will make these evil ones pay. An eye for an eye, a tooth for a tooth. He pressed down on the

127

accelerator and closed the gap between his own car
and the monsignor's. Let him experience fear. Yes,
that's what I intend for the monsignor. Fear!

Monsignor Fallon almost swore out loud. If he'd been
accustomed to using swear words when angry, he'd
have done so. He pounded the steering wheel and
screamed: *damn! damn! damn!.* The high beams
penetrated his car, reflecting off his mirrors and
distracting him. He was annoyed. Why would
someone follow him? He had no enemies. And he
had no money. They'd get nothing if they robbed
him. Maybe I can lose him, he thought. He pushed
down on the accelerator and watched the needle move
from sixty to sixty-five to seventy. He didn't feel safe
at this speed, especially now that it was dark, but he
had to try and get away. It had started to rain and
his windscreen fogged up. He strained to see as the
high beams behind continued to drill into him.
Maybe I should get off the road, he thought. The
village of Cong lay a mile ahead and he decided to
stop and seek refuge there.
        Losing his concentration, he suddenly realized
that the speedometer needle was nudging seventy-
five as he entered the village of Cong. He hit the
brakes and tried to slow down. But the rain had
slicked the ground and he missed his turn-off into the
main street of the village. The car spun out of
control, almost hitting the dark limestone plinth of
the Market Cross, and crossed the street at an angle
narrowly missing the corner houses on each side until
it finally slid into the old wall surrounding Cong
Abbey. Steam rose out of the radiator and the bonnet
had crumpled like a piece of cheap tin. The adrenalin
was telling him to flee and the seat belts were cutting
into his neck and shoulder telling him not to move.

He released the seat belt and looked over his shoulder to see the street in darkness behind him. No sign of the car that had followed him. Maybe this is God's will that I should come to the Abbey on a night like this. Fumbling under the seat, he found a flashlight he'd stowed there. Hoping that the batteries still worked, he turned it on. It shone but dimly. The batteries were on their last legs. It wouldn't last long. The rain had eased off and he made a decision. He'd visit the Abbey and pray. Then he'd find somewhere to stay for the night and get a garage to take care of his car in the morning.

Pulling the hood of his raincoat over his head, he had enough street light to let him see the entrance to the abbey, a few yards ahead. Founded by the last High King of Ireland, Turlough O'Conor, in the early twelfth century for the Augustinians, its ruined walls still stood, a monument to its grandeur. Passing through its very beautiful doorway, he turned the flashlight on and briefly illuminated the intricate carvings that framed it. Even though he'd been there many times before, he was still in awe of the artistry.

He stepped through the doorway and stood inside the great abbey church. The rain had stopped and the sky now served as a huge vaulted roof. He felt the majesty of God here and, using the flashlight, stepped over the tombstones that paved the floor until he reached the centre. Kneeling then, he clasped his hands in silent prayer.

The sound of footsteps on gravel brought him out of his reverie of prayer in time to see the rays of a very powerful flashlight streak across the walls at the gable end. Painfully, he forced his arthritic hips to support his legs as he stood. But the flashlight, almost a searchlight had now found him and he stood there in its glow.

"Monsignor, so good of you to wait for me."
The voice was strong, even theatrical, with a strong
sense of threat.

"Who are you? What do you want with me?"

"It doesn't matter who I am. It's God who
wants you, wants a reckoning with you."

That was enough for the Monsignor. This
man sounded deranged. He'd have to get away from
him. So he turned and ran, stumbling over the large
flat tombstones. If he could make it to the forest at
the end of the open cloisters, he might be able to hide.
He knew the direction but he couldn't see and his
flashlight was almost dead. But he could see more
from the powerful light that his pursuer splayed back
and forth. He dashed ahead, then tripped and fell,
the flashlight clattering away from him. Hurting
badly, he got up again and finally made it though the
church wall into the cloisters at the rear. He knew
that if he followed the path straight ahead, it would
lead him into the dense Ashford forest where he
might be able to hide.

He could sense his pursuer closing in so he
started to run, blindly, tripped and fell almost
immediately. Stunned, he tried to get up but couldn't.
Then he felt strong hands behind him, lifting him
and holding him. He was powerless to fight back as
he felt some kind of restraints tying his wrists
together behind his back. His attacker said nothing.
Monsignor Fallon fell back on the only defence he
knew: prayer. He prayed as his attacker pulled and
dragged him down the pathway between the trees
until they reached the river. He couldn't see it clearly
but he could hear the rush of its water.

The Avenger knew what he must do. But he wanted the monsignor to know why. He wanted to give him time to repent before he met his God. An old abandoned stone house, the walls still standing, stood out over the river. Used as a fish house by the friars, it was constructed over the river to trap the fish in a crib underneath. Swimming about they touched a wire that rang a bell to let the cook know. The Avenger thought that the old fish house would do nicely. Dragging the monsignor onto it, he looped a rope through the restraints on his wrist and pushed him over the edge until he was waist deep in the river. He tied the rope around a metal_barrier that had been installed to protect the tourists and stood up. The monsignor had said nothing, only prayed all the time, and now prayed even louder. He took the bible out of his pocket, held the flashlight over it, and in his deep theatrical voice, started to read:

"Monsignor, you must already know why you are here. You must know the crimes you have committed. No? You do not defend yourself. Yes, go on, pray. Maybe the Lord will forgive you. After all he is compassionate, we think."

"But I will read from the bible so you can listen to his anger"

In Jude 1:7, *the Lord says that "Sodom and Gomorrah and the surrounding towns gave themselves up to sexual immorality and perversion"*

Monsignor Fallon had stopped praying and was trying to speak. But only phlegm and grunts emitted from his mouth. He could not utter any words. His tongue failed him and he could feel his heart racing and then skipping and stopping and spluttering. He could hear his torturer's voice clearly and it seemed familiar to him. But he believed that

131

he was only imagining that. He tried to speak again but his larynx had shut down.

"And, Monsignor, you and those like you are no better than the people of Sodom and Gomorrah! I see you trying to speak but the Lord won't let you defend yourself. No, there is no defence for you. You are guilty. And what punishment does the Lord dictate?"

"He says, *'If your right eye makes you do wrong, take it out and throw it away. It is better to lose a part of your body, than for your whole body to be thrown into hell. If your hand or your foot makes you do wrong, cut it off and throw it away! It is better for you to enter into life without hands or feet than to have two hands and two feet and be thrown into the fire that burns for ever.'* "

"And what does he tell us to do? You must know the answer."

"He tells us to *'take the man or woman who has done this evil deed to your city gate and stone that person to death'* "

"But I will leave you here like this and if the Lord has compassion he will save you!"

The water now lapped over the monsignor's chest and he no longer felt anything in his legs. Before he lapsed into unconsciousness, something screamed in his brain "I know that voice! I know who he is."

The Avenger left Cong in a state of numbness. He did not feel any remorse. He never felt remorse. Driving with his right hand he fingered his rosary beads in his left. He wasn't saying the rosary. He mostly used the beads as a touchstone, a comforter, a

132

device to control his emotions. He knew that he was God's instrument. God had asked him to clear out the temple, to pluck out the eyes that offended, to cut off the hands that scandalized. His work had only just begun. He inserted the CD of Biscantorat and hit the play button. Adjusting the volume, he almost closed his eyes as The Sound of The Spirit from Glenstal Abbey *filled the air*

The music soothed him and he began to relax. As the car warmed up, the tension and anger left his body and he could feel himself become Father Bernard Flaherty again.

The chapel appeared like a ship in the mist. A triangular shape, beached on the mountainy roadside, buffeted by the rain and wind, the invitation *Stop and Pray,* black on white, glared at Father Bernard Flaherty in the headlights of his car.

He pulled into the small empty parking place in front of the church. One light shone inside through the large transparent front windows. He sat for a while, then got out, pulled the hood of his coat over his head, and strode through the rain to the front door. It was open. He entered and looked around. Empty, as though it had been reserved especially for him. For a brief moment, he wondered if this church really existed, wondered if it would really be here if he drove past in tomorrow's daylight.

He walked slowly up the centre aisle until he reached the altar rail. Without hesitation, he knelt and let his wet raincoat drop to the ground at his feet, puddles of rainwater soon accumulating on the tiles that surrounded him.

And he prayed.

"Dear Lord, I did not ask for this. Just as you did not ask for the suffering you endured, for the

brutal crucifixion, so I have not asked to be your instrument of vengeance. But your church on earth must be cleansed of its sins. Your people must see that the will of God is carried out. Your people will know the signs. They will know that these defilers have been punished by you. They will know the signs. Just as you prophesized against the Philistines when you promised that you would stretch out your hand against them, carry out great vengeance on them and punish them in your wrath. They knew that you were the Lord when you took vengeance on them."

Slowly he rose to his feet, raised the raincoat from the floor and pulled it around his shoulders. He genuflected, turned around and walked briskly out of the church. The rain had turned to a fine drizzle, peppering his face and filling him with renewed energy. He felt cleansed, refreshed, his soul blessed by God. He climbed into his car and headed towards Athlone. It was Easter holidays at St. Curnan's and he wasn't expected back for two weeks. Enough time to let the news about the monsignor get absorbed in his absence.

He headed for the monastery in Mullingar. They were expecting him and he would be able to find solace there. And await the word of the Lord.

Under the Bougainvillea

As I said in my introduction: '*Some of these are so short that I see them as vignettes of life, those slices of life that often have no beginning or middle, but do have an end. **Under the Bougainvillea** is a good example.*'

It was originally published in the ***Electric Acorn eZine*** of ***The Dublin Writers' Workshop.***

ENDINGS   Pat Mullan

Miami, Florida

The bougainvillea had started to flower again, a deep fuchsia color. It climbed the wall of their patio until it reached the second floor where it clambered around the metal railings on their bedroom window.

  Bloom lay in bed looking out of that window, seeing the bougainvillea frame a picture of two golfers at the fifth tee. He wasn't a golfer himself and he often wondered why he had chosen to live in the middle of a golf course. But he had to remind himself that he hadn't made the choice alone. They had made it together. She said that it would be better than living over on the beach or downtown. At least he was closer to the office here and they could use the golf course for their morning walks. Besides, she said it would be nice to be able to look out on the green grass.

  Idyllic. That's the way it was supposed to be. Or that's the way she pretended it would be. Here they could forget the past and start over again. But that had been wishful thinking. They couldn't leave the past behind. It was part of them. Where they went, it went too.

  . "It's your drinking that's destroying us," she said, one afternoon after he'd staggered in at 3 am the night before. They were sitting on the beach near the lighthouse on Key Biscayne, one of the places they went when they wanted to escape from Miami

137

. "I'm going to stop. I promise," said Bloom.

"How many times have you said that? How many?" The despair in her voice twanged the nerves in his already hung-over head. He wanted to hurt her. He couldn't stop himself.

"Why am I drinking like this? You tell me. Go on, tell me!" Bloom's voice was too hoarse for the scream and the words left his throat in a painful screech.

Meg said nothing. This was old territory. They'd been here before. Too many times. She couldn't take back the past. She couldn't undo the damage. And she had never forgiven herself. Maybe if I'd been able to forgive myself, she thought, then maybe I'd have been able to stop him from trying to destroy himself.

They had met in Paris. Five years ago. He was there on business, glad to be away from the States and the end of a marriage that had never worked. She was living in Paris, working for a French company, and reveling in her romance with the language. But she was on a journey. Fleeing from an abusive relationship and running east. A month later she would have been in Hong Kong. Such is fate.

They were both American but from entirely different backgrounds. She was Boston Irish and he was Brooklyn Jewish. She used to remind him, in those lighthearted days, that one of the most famous Irishmen was Leopold Bloom. They shared a love of literature and the arts, spending hours in the Louvre and afternoons in cafes and bookstores, often losing all sense of time among the shelves of Shakespeare & Co. Evenings on the left bank, chocolate crepes on the street, good wine, and great times in bed. Days of wine and roses. They saw the Lee Remick and Jack Lemmon film and they knew that it could have been them up there on that screen. But work and career saved them from a life of dissolution in Paris. Bloom was posted back to the States. A month later Meg joined him.

Idyllic. Yes, for the first few months in Miami their life was indeed idyllic. A new world, an exotic Latin city in the heart of the South. They explored every inch of it together, preferring to eat where the Cubans ate, on Calle Ocho, and getting away to Key West whenever they could for a long weekend. Hanging out in Sloppy Joe's, Hemingway's bar. Bloom had once had dreams of being a writer. But he had never done anything about it. In Sloppy Joe's he fantasized that Hemingway's muse might strike. It didn't. The only thing that struck him was the massive hang-over the following day from too many margaritas.

They left the lighthouse at Key Biscayne with nothing resolved. How could it be? On the way home Meg fought back the memory of when it had all begun to collapse. Bloom had been gone for a week on business and his very best friend had promised to look after Meg in his absence. Oh, yes, he had looked after me all right, thought Meg. She was vulnerable and lonely and he had taken advantage of that. Great wine and a romantic atmosphere can lead to anything, even to throwing caution to the winds. And Meg had slept with him. In Bloom's close circle there was never going to be a way to keep that secret. And so he found out and confronted her. Maybe she should have lied. But she didn't. She admitted it and asked to be forgiven. Instead Bloom hit the bottle.

Real hard. And their life had been going downhill ever since.

Watching the golfers as the balmy Miami breezes wafted through the bedroom window, Bloom realized how tired he felt. No wonder. He'd 'tied one on' last night again. He had no memory of getting home. Another blackout. That scared him. But, in a perverse way, it protected him from embarrassing memories. He looked over at the other side of their king-size bed. Didn't look like Meg had slept there very much last night. He didn't hear her downstairs and he reckoned that she'd probably gone to the beach or the health club. Anything but having to face him. Gradually the tiredness overcame him and sleep closed in.

He was dreaming and, somehow, he knew he was dreaming.... They were having a huge fight. She said she was leaving him. This was the end. No more. He was drunk. He knew he was drunk but he was in a rage. An uncontrollable rage. He knew that too. She ran upstairs and locked herself in the bedroom and refused to let him in. That infuriated him even more. So he charged the door with his shoulder, his feet, and anything that he could lay his hands on. The door fractured around the lock and gave way. He charged into the bedroom and she fled out past him. He turned and rushed towards her, forcing her onto the edge of the stairs. She lost her balance. He reached for her and missed. She tumbled down the stairs, never uttering a word, and lay in a crumpled heap at the bottom.

Bloom woke up in a cold sweat. Terrified. He told himself that was it. No more booze. I'm losing my mind.

He decided to get up and head for the shower. On his way there he noticed that the bedroom door seemed off-balance. That's odd, he thought. He tried to close the door and that's when he saw the fracture around the lock. He froze right there. Hoping against hope that his dream had only been a nightmare, he moved to the stairs and looked down.

Meg's body lay, in a crumpled heap, at the bottom of the stairs. Shocked, he felt dizzy and weak.

Numb, he crept down the stairs, clinging to each rung, one step at a time.

He knelt beside Meg. He could see, from the twisted way she lay, that her neck was broken. No point in checking for a pulse. But he did anyway. Hoping for a miracle.

He cried, loudly and painfully, until his lungs hurt. and then sobbed and sobbed until he was drained.

Finally he gently placed a duvet over her and picked up the phone and dialed the Miami Dade Police Department.

Then he went out to the patio, sat down under the bougainvillea, and watched the next group of golfers at the fifth tee.

And waited.

ENDINGS   Pat Mullan

You Always Wondered

You Always Wondered is truly a vignette of life. It explores the tragedy and poignancy of loss. It deals with the end of life, an unexpected ending. Originally written with no context in mind, it has since found its way into *Childhood Hills* and then into *Blood Red Square* where it showed Owen MacDara mourning over the loss of his wife.

And so it seems perfectly suitable as an *ending* for *Endings*.

ENDINGS   Pat Mullan

You Always Wondered

You know there was no-one in the bedroom when you felt your way in the darkness to the toilet. They say there's a cold feeling in the air when there's another presence in the room but you convinced yourself that it was natural to feel a cold chill in January.

She didn't stir on her side of the bed. You always woke up quietly. You always slid your feet out onto the cold floor and eased the rest of your body out without tugging the bedclothes. She never knew that you went to the toilet three times during the night. You never told her. You didn't want her to know that your body was beginning to show the signs of wear.

You never flushed the toilet at night. The filling tank made too much noise. It would surely wake her up. She always left her watch on the glass shelf by the sink. That's the only way you knew the time. But you really didn't want to know the time. You always left your own watch on the side table by your bed, in the dark where you couldn't read it till daybreak.

You groped behind you with your right hand and found the hot water bottle that she had put in your side of the bed. It was tepid now at three in the morning. You slid under the duvet and pulled it up so that your head was covered, just enough to hide you but not enough to suffocate you. You turned over on

145

your left side so that your good left ear was silenced by the pillow. Your deaf right ear didn't matter.

You lay there as you did every night, trying to get back to sleep. Eventually you did return to sleep but never to the dream you were in before you woke up.

She was always awake before you. You would wake up to the feeling of her arm around your waist, her loins warm against the small of your back and her lips brushing the nape of your neck. You always turned over and blessed your good fortune as your arms encircled her body and you kissed her gently on her eyelids, the tip of her nose, and her soft inviting lips.

You always wondered what she would do that morning when you didn't respond. That morning you were certain would come when she would wake up, stretch and turn around to encircle your waist and brush her lips against your cold, cold neck. That morning when you wouldn't turn over to hold her. That last morning of your life. You always wondered about that.

You were still wondering when you realized you were awake. It was morning and the light was filtering into the bedroom. You had wakened by yourself this morning. You turned and looked over. She was still asleep. You felt as though you had been given a gift today. The gift of morning that she always brought to you. You would bring it to her.

You turned over and circled her waist with your arm. You brushed your lips against her cold, cold neck.

ENDINGS

Pat Mullan

ENDINGS   Pat Mullan

Pat Mullan

Pat Mullan is a thriller writer, poet, and artist. He was born in Ireland and has lived in England, Canada and the USA. He now lives in Connemara, in the west of Ireland.

You can visit him at: www.patmullan.com

ENDINGS   Pat Mullan

Other works by Pat Mullan:

THRILLERS

The Circle of Sodom:
http://amzn.to/15WQNgQ

Blood Red Square
http://amzn.to/189ZWBS

Last Days of The Tiger
http://amzn.to/16I2DJi

Creatures of Habit
http://amzn.to/WBCqFK

POETRY

Childhood Hills:
http://amzn.to/1000L9P

Awakening
http://amzn.to/10pyEji

James Dickey's Poetry:
The Religious Dimension
http://amzn.to/YjnaDM

Knowing
http://amzn.to/18ir14O

SHORT WORK

Galway Girl
http://amzn.to/X2lkDa

Tribunal
http://amzn.to/10022xq

Screwed
http://amzn.to/11SRzY2

The Avenger
http://amzn.to/156S05x

Facsimile
http://amzn.to/156SgBN

Galway Noir
http://bit.ly/ZTy8OK

Eleven Days in July
http://amzn.to/12X499z

ENDINGS   Pat Mullan

ENDINGS

Pat Mullan

ENDINGS   Pat Mullan

www.ingramcontent.com/pod-product-compliance
Lightning Source LLC
Chambersburg PA
CBHW021109130626
46554CB00002B/603